Courting in Colorado

Book 27 in At the Altar

Kirsten Osbourne

Chapter One

Alexis groaned as her phone rang at the ungodly hour of ten in the morning. She worked all night doing customer service in a call center, and a call between the hours of eight am and four pm was sure to wake her.

She reached over and took her phone from her nightstand, squinting to try to see exactly who was calling. It was a number she didn't recognize. "Hello?" she asked, knowing her voice would sound sleepy to whoever was on the other end.

"Miss Paxton?" a man's voice asked.

"Yes, this is she." Alexis forced herself to sit up, so she wouldn't fall back to sleep and start snoring in the man's ear.

"I'm the attorney for your late father."

"My father?" She'd just seen him the weekend before. He was fine. "What's happened?"

"He was thrown from his horse and broke his neck. I need you to come to Boulder for the reading of the will."

Alexis frowned. "My father doesn't ride horses. He's a pharmacist here in Texas. Why would I go to Boulder?"

"Alexander Tobias was never a pharmacist. He's a rancher outside of Boulder. The will needs to be read on Monday morning, and you must be here. I'll text you the details, including the address and time."

"All right." She had no idea what was happening. When the call ended, she stared at her phone for a moment and then called her mother.

"Hi, sweetie! Shouldn't you be sleeping?"

"Mom, I just got a really strange phone call."

"Strange enough that you're calling me while you should be sleeping?"

"Yes. A man just called and told me my father died, and he's the attorney for him. A man named Alexander Tobias. I know it must be some mistake, but...I'm supposed to be there for the reading of the will on Monday."

There was silence for a moment on the other end of the call. "It's not a mistake," her mother finally said. "I never meant for you to find out this way."

"So Dad isn't my father?" This morning was making less and less sense to her.

"No, he's not. I married him when you were still a baby, and he adopted you. Your biological father is...or I guess was...Alexander Tobias."

"I'm on my way. I need full details." Alexis had no real desire to dig anymore. She was already reeling from the information she'd been given, but she knew she needed to learn as much as she could before Monday.

She no longer had any thoughts of sleeping and called into work. It was Friday morning, and she was due to work from nine to six overnight. She didn't think there was any way she could do that at this point. She let them know her father had died, and she'd be out for a few days.

She pulled on an old pair of shorts and a tank top and rushed out to her car. Her mother lived just a short distance away, but it was August in Texas, and though she would walk if the weather was better, she wasn't about to do it in ninety-eight-degree heat.

She pulled into her parents' driveway and just stared at the house she'd grown up in. Slowly, she got out of the car and walked into the house, not bothering to knock. "Mom! I'm here!" she called out, and her mother walked to her and hugged her.

"What in the world is going on? If I'm adopted, why was I never told? Didn't my father want visitation rights?"

It was hard to think of anyone but Brad Paxton as her father, but she didn't know how else to refer to the man who had just died.

"Come into the living room. I saved some stuff for you so I could tell you one day. I don't know why I never did. Brad always told me I should be honest."

Alexis followed her mother into the living room, sitting beside her on the couch. On the coffee table was what looked to be a scrapbook. She reached for it. It was certainly one she'd never seen.

Her mother started talking as she touched the cover.

"When I was nineteen, I met a man who walked into my father's restaurant. I was waiting tables after school, and this man... Well, he was a tall, handsome rancher. I waited on him, and he came in every day for a week. I was young, and I flirted, and he flirted, and at the end of the week, he said he had to go home to Colorado."

Alexis nodded. "And?"

"And he asked me to go to Colorado with him as his wife." Mom shook her head. "For a short while I thought he was insane, but the more we talked, the more I liked him. We had a long-distance thing going for a month or two, and my parents hated the idea of me marrying him."

"I'm sure," Alexis said. Her grandparents still owned the restaurant her mother had mentioned, and she'd spent many hours there herself waiting tables.

"But I decided that we were meant to be together. So, I agreed to marry him, and I drove my car with everything I owned to Boulder, Colorado and we were married the day I arrived. I thought it was so romantic to leave everyone and everything I'd ever loved and marry this man."

"But it wasn't?" Alexis asked.

"Oh, it was. And he was a good man, who doted on me. I got pregnant after a few months, and I started to miss my mother. I wanted her with me as all these changes were happening to my body. She couldn't take time away from the restaurant though, and I got depressed in Colorado, home all day with no one but the housekeeper to talk to, and I didn't much like the housekeeper. I'd call Mom all hours of the day and night, simply for someone to talk to."

"Sounds like you were miserable."

"I was, but it wasn't about Alex. I loved him, as much as a young girl who knows nothing about love can." Mom shook her head. "But as I was getting closer to having you, I decided to come back here to have you, so my mother could be with me.

"Alex didn't want me to go, but I insisted, and in the end, he agreed. So, I moved back in with my parents, who had never liked Alex to begin with. We'd talk on the phone for a bit every day, but things were different. Living with him no longer sounded romantic, and I felt better having my friends and family around me. Finally, while we were talking one night, I told him I didn't think I could go back. I was so much happier here. I suggested he sell his ranch and move here, where he could start a new ranch. He said his ranch had been in his family for more than a hundred years, and he wasn't moving. By the time you were born, we were in the process of getting divorced."

"But that's silly! Why didn't you fight for your love?"

"Because what I felt wasn't truly love. I never missed him the way I missed my parents and friends." Mom sighed, looking down at her hands for a moment. "I met Brad when you got sick when you were just a few weeks old. I took the prescription to his pharmacy, and he filled it. We talked, and I agreed to go out with him." She shrugged. "He knew I was getting a divorce and I had a tiny baby. He didn't care. We married five days after the divorce was final. Alex gave up his parental rights, not wanting you torn between him and me. Brad adopted you when you were a year old."

"But...why didn't you ever tell me?"

Mom shook her head. "By the time you were old enough, we'd had the twins," she said, speaking of her brother and sister who were two years younger than Alexis. "I never wanted you to feel like you were less loved than they were because you had a different father. You all grew up, and I thought I should tell you so many times, but I never felt it was important enough to actually do it. And now you found out, and I realize I was wrong the whole time."

Alexis closed her eyes for a moment, wanting to yell at her mother, but she knew it would only hurt her. There was no reason to do that. "I see."

Her mother reached for the scrapbook, opening it to the first page. "That was his receipt from his first meal at the restaurant. He was here to find some bulls for his herd." Turning the page, she showed Alexis a copy of their marriage license.

As she flipped through the book, Alexis saw a whole marriage, which had ended much too soon. "I think it would have been good for you to get to know your father, and Brad and I talked about sending you to spend a summer with him many times. I even arranged it all with Alex, but in the end, I chickened out. I'm sure you realize that you were named after him. He was Alexander Thomas Tobias."

"That's where you got Thomasina from. I thought you hated me for years because you gave me that horrible middle name."

Her mother laughed. "Your middle name is a small act of kindness toward the man who gave you life. He's always known what you were doing. He got your school picture every year, and I'd send him snapshots of you taken at different places. He always got a copy of your report card, and he even paid for half of your college education. We didn't need him to, but he was so excited you were going to college that he insisted."

"He sounds like a really good man."

"He was a better man than anyone but maybe Brad. Not seeing you was very hard for him, but he always wanted what was best for you. He'd send you Christmas and birthday presents, and I always gave them to you from your great aunt Alice."

"I wondered why I never met her!" Alexis shook her head. "So he bought my first computer. My first phone. I thought Alice was the most wonderful aunt in the whole wide world!"

Her mother laughed. "It was all Alex. I didn't want to claim I was giving you the gifts, and I would buy small gifts for Brent and Brittany from her, so they wouldn't feel left out."

"Do they know?" Alexis asked.

Her mother shook her head. "Your grandparents and Brad and I know. No one else."

"And now I have to go for the reading of the will of a man I never met, but who took such an interest in my life. I don't know how to do this."

"You just go. It's fine. Do you need money for the plane tickets?" she asked.

Alexis frowned. She hadn't thought about getting there. "I think I'm fine."

"Do you hate me?"

Alexis shook her head. "How could I hate you? You did what you thought was best, I'm sure, just as Dad did. And just as Alex did. How could I be upset that I had so many people loving me? I wish you'd told me, but I think I understand why you didn't." And she wasn't angry, but she did feel as if she'd been robbed of a loving father. "I'm going to go home, get a little sleep, and arrange to fly out there on Sunday evening."

Her mother hugged her again. "If you have any questions about him, I'm happy to answer," Mom said as she headed for the door.

"Thanks for that," Alexis said. "And you should tell Brent and Brittany. They have a right to know."

As soon as she got home, Alexis looked up Boulder, Colorado, and typed in her father's name. It looked like he'd never remarried, but he was very active and very generous. There were pictures of his ranch, and she shook her head, wondering about what he would have been like had they been together. She'd never know now.

She booked her ticket for Sunday afternoon, and she planned to return on Tuesday. She wanted to at least see his ranch, where her mother had once lived, and her father had always lived.

She couldn't believe how much her life had changed in the space of a few hours, but hopefully, it would be a change for the better.

AT TEN ON MONDAY MORNING, Alexis sat in a small room with an elderly woman, a lawyer, and two men who looked like cowboys. She was nervous, not knowing anyone. She wished she'd asked her mother to accompany her on the trip, but she understood why her mother hadn't volunteered.

After what seemed like forever, the lawyer picked up a paper and began to read. "To Mildred Garvonovich, my housekeeper of many years, I leave the house she resides in on my ranch and five hundred thousand dollars to use as she pleases. Upon her death, the house will revert to the ranch. To Joe Cahill, I leave five hundred thousand dollars, and the same to Adam Porter. To my daughter, Alexis Paxton, I leave my ranch, provided she agree to live there and make sure it is run properly, otherwise it will go to Joe Cahill and Adam Porter, who will run it together. Also to my daughter, I leave the contents of my home and all of the funds I have that have not been listed."

The lawyer looked up. "I also have a letter for you, Alexis."

Alexis nodded, feeling very conspicuous. She didn't belong in this room with people who loved her father. She hadn't known he existed.

After the others had left the room, he handed her the letter that her father had written to her.

My dear Alexis,

I know my very existence must be a shock to you, but I have loved you from afar your entire life. I was there when you graduated from high school, cheering for you every moment of it. I was there for your college graduation, and I was there when you were in your school play and you were Dorcas in Seven Brides for Seven Brothers. I'm so proud of you for getting your degree in business management, and I confess that I asked your mother to encourage you to make that your degree so that you would one day have the knowledge to run my ranch. I pray that you'll find yourself a cowboy who can take care of the everyday operations of the ranch, while you take care of the business end of things.

I love you with everything inside me, and I hope that you'll stay and run the ranch that has been in our family for generations. You're the last Tobias to take it over, and I know you'll make me proud, like you've been doing since you took your first steps.

Your father,

Alexander Thomas Tobias

After finishing the letter, Alexis had tears streaming down her face. "I wish I could have met him."

The lawyer nodded. "I do too. He was a wonderful man." He pushed something toward her across his desk. "I took the liberty of trying to find a way for you to meet a man who could run your ranch, and I found this woman's name. She runs a matchmaking service where people are introduced at the altar. I hope you'll give her a call and tell her just what you need in a husband."

Alexis took the paper, unsure if she would call. "Am I allowed to drive out and see the ranch?" she asked.

"Allowed? You're encouraged to do so. It's yours. There's always a key hidden under the turtle on the front porch."

She nodded, and left the room, wondering what on earth a city girl like her was going to do with a ranch.

Chapter Two

According to Google, the ranch was about twenty minutes out of town, and she set up the navigation on the rental car she was in and drove out to see what was there. She drove through a gate that read, "Tobias Ranch," and she parked right in front of the house. When she tried the door, it was locked, so she found the key under the turtle and opened the door.

The house was huge and though it looked like it was very well constructed, it was furnished the way she would expect a rancher's home to look. As she walked into the living room, she saw pictures of herself looking at her from every direction.

She explored, finding six bedrooms, three up and three down, each with a bathroom attached. There were even guest baths peppered in different places. The kitchen was a cook's dream, and she did love to cook. There were two wall ovens, one above the other, and a stove with six spots to cook.

Everything about this house screamed "home" to her in a way that her mother's house in Arlington never had. This place...she wanted to live here with every fiber of her being. But living here meant running the ranch, and she'd never been on a horse and had only been close to cows at the petting zoo that was part of the Fort Worth Zoo.

Walking back to the living room, she sat down, and called the number that was on the paper the lawyer had given her. It was time to act. "This is Dr. Lachele!"

"Uh, yes. This is Alexis Paxton. I want you to find me a cowboy to marry."

There was laughter on the other end of the phone. "Do you think he'll look good in his Wranglers?"

"I hope so," Alexis responded, smiling. "I just lost a father, I didn't know existed, and I have inherited his ranch in Colorado. I need to marry someone who can help me run it. I know business, and I'll work on that aspect of things, but I need someone who knows how to run a ranch alongside me."

"Where do you live, sugar?"

"I live in Arlington, TX, but I'm inheriting the ranch in Boulder, Colorado. I'd like to marry soon."

"I'll need to do some psychological testing, and that will have to take place at your home. Does that work for you?"

Alexis thought for a minute. "You know what? Let's meet at my ranch. Where are you?"

"I'm in Manhattan, but I'll come to you, sweetie. Just give me an address. Would Saturday work for you?"

"Yes, it should." Alexis's mind was going a mile a minute, thinking about everything she would need to do to make the move to Colorado.

"All right. The tests take about eight hours. Just text me at this same number with the address of the ranch, and I'll see you on Saturday morning."

Alexis was surprised that the call ended. "Well, I guess that's set up." She called her supervisor. "I know this is going to sound crazy, but I just inherited a ranch in Colorado from a father I didn't know existed. I'm going to take over the ranch, and I won't be back to work."

"Seriously?" Amanda asked.

"Yes," Alexis said. "I need to do what he would have wanted me to do."

"All right. I'll mail your stuff to you. Should I send it to your apartment?"

"No, send it here." Alexis rattled off the address. "Thank you for understanding!"

"Oh, no problem there. I would trade my job for a ranch any day."

"Just because you like to see men's butts in Wranglers," Alexis said, grinning. The other woman would be much more suited to taking over a ranch than she would.

"So true! Stay in touch!"

"I'll try!"

Alexis got up and went into the bedroom that had obviously been her father's. She went into the closet and looked at his clothes, making piles of things to donate and things to throw away. Someone would be able to use his charcoal gray suit that looked as if it had been worn once. The repeatedly patched jeans were another story.

She realized it would be a lot of work to go through everything and decide if she should keep it or sell it, but it had to be done.

After calling her mother, and letting her know what had happened, Alexis said, "I think I'm going to stay here."

"I had a feeling you'd feel that way after seeing the ranch. I've always seen so much of your father in you."

"I also contacted a matchmaker who introduces people at the altar. I asked her to set me up with a cowboy who could handle day-to-day operations, while I handle the business side of things. I hope you'll come when I have a wedding date."

Mom laughed softly. "Of course I will, and I'll drag your father, sister, and brother along with me."

"Perfect. I love you."

"I love you too, LexiLou."

"I believe that's Lexi Thomasina to you," Alexis said as she hung up the phone. She would meet with Dr. Lachele, and then she'd fly home and pack her things up. She had to get her car anyway. It was going to be a busy few weeks.

When Dr. Lachele arrived Saturday morning, she was not what Alexis had expected. Anyone with Dr. in front of their name shouldn't have purple hair, should they? It was just strange.

She enjoyed the interview process, feeling as if she'd made a new lifelong friend in the process.

Dr. Lachele smiled more and more as the day went on. Before she left, she said, "I have a man in mind for you, and he would happily relocate. I think I can have you married off in two weeks."

"That fast?" Alexis asked, surprised.

"Yes, that fast. But you need someone fast, so it will be good."

Alexis nodded, feeling a bit uncertain. "Let's do it!"

After she was gone, Alexis thought about everything that had happened that week. She'd gotten into her father's computer, and she could see his bookkeeping was meticulous. She could easily work with his figures.

The foreman, Joe Cahill, who she'd met at the reading of the will had met with her a few times to let her know what was happening on the ranch. He told her he'd work for her for two months, and then he was retiring.

She didn't blame him, but that had made her time crunch a little more serious than it had been.

She flew home Sunday and arranged for all of her things to be either shipped to Colorado or donated to charity. Back at the ranch on Monday, she knew she needed to start things how she meant to go on.

And that meant going through more and more of the things in the house and deciding what was staying, what was being sold, and what was being donated.

ALEXIS'S MOTHER FLEW out a week before the wedding, and she helped her find a dress and work out a few details. She'd decided to be married in the church her father had been a member of, and it felt good to do so.

As her mother walked through the house, she'd been surprised at how little had changed. "The major difference is all the pictures of you," she said, shaking her head. "He was a man who didn't like change much."

The day before the wedding her entire family joined them at the ranch, planning to fly out after the wedding, so she would have a house full of people one day and they'd be gone the next. That felt quite odd to her.

She and her sister sat with their mother at the back of the church on her wedding day. They'd found a beautiful wedding gown, and her mother had been able to fit it to her in no time. "I'm so happy for clearance," Alexis said.

"Are you nervous?" Brittany asked. "I mean, you're marrying someone you've never met and know nothing about."

"I know he's a cowboy," Alexis said. "That's my only requirement at the moment. A cowboy who can run the ranch."

"Just think, two weeks ago, you were on the phones all night, wearing an ugly thing on your head. Now, you own and operate your own multi-million dollar ranch. It doesn't seem possible."

"I agree!" Alexis said. "I guess when you find your birth father, your life will change too."

Brittany laughed, but Mom gave them both a disgusted look. "No more jokes about fathers coming out of nowhere. You two have a ridiculous sense of humor."

Alexis and Brittany looked at one another and giggled again. "Sorry, Mom," Alexis said.

Dr. Lachele came into the room then. "There's my favorite bride," she said, grinning at Alexis.

"Hi, Dr. Lachele. Is my hero wearing his cowboy hat?"

"Your hero?" Dr. Lachele asked.

"I'm living a romance novel about my own life, so whomever I marry will be my hero."

"I approve," Dr. Lachele said. "Do you need anything?"

Alexis shook her head. "Not at all. If he passed your tests, then I know he's not a deranged psycho-killer there to murder me in my sleep."

Her mother glared. "Alexis Thomasina! You need to calm down a bit."

"I can't! I drank way too much coffee this morning because I didn't sleep last night. I think I'm going to crash hard later."

Dr. Lachele shook her head. "She's doing just fine, Mrs. Paxton."

"You only say that because you didn't raise her, and you don't know that she is perfectly capable of acting like an adult."

"Well, I think she's absolutely perfect, and I know of a cowboy who will share that opinion." Dr. Lachele glanced at her watch. "It's time. I feel like I should clap my hands and say, 'Places everyone!'"

"Do it!" Alexis told her. "It would make me so happy!"

Mom once again frowned at Alexis, but Alexis wasn't terribly bothered. Brittany thought she was funny.

Soon, Alexis was at the back of the church with her hand on her father's arm, ready to walk down the aisle. "Do we have a code if he isn't worth marrying?"

Alexis giggled but shook her head. "No jokes around Mom today. Brittany and I wore her out."

He laughed. "I will endeavor to do my best."

As they slowly walked down the aisle to a man with dark hair and eyes, wearing a black cowboy hat to match his suit, Alexis felt a sense of peace wash over her. She was doing the riskiest thing she'd ever done in her life, and it felt so right. Soon she'd be married, and then her life would really start.

When she reached the front of the church, she gave her groom her best smile as her father put her hand into his.

Alexis gripped the new hand tightly as if to let him know they would be unified against the world. She doubted he got that from her hand, but if he did, she'd know they were perfect for each other.

The pastor started the ceremony. "We are gathered here today to join this woman, Alexis Paxton, with this man, Kyle Stifter, in holy matrimony."

After that, she mostly spaced out. She repeated her vows when she was supposed to and held her hand out for the ring at the appropriate time. When he was told to kiss his bride, he barely brushed his lips against hers. She was a bit disappointed and wanted to know what his problem was, but she'd ask that later.

Or maybe soon. She would be asking though.

She'd decided against a reception because she didn't know anyone in the area, and they were going to lunch with her family instead before the family left for the airport. As she walked with Kyle to the back of the church, she softly explained that. "And what was with the kiss? That wasn't a kiss. That was the kind of kiss you give your puppy for being sweet."

He chuckled. "It was meant to be. I want to have our first real kiss with no observers. Why should the whole world get to be there for everything?"

"I guess that's all right then. Tell me about yourself. I assume you're a cowboy. Does that mean you're ready to run the day-to-day operations of my ranch?"

He stopped walking. "What?"

"I forget. You know exactly as much about me as I know about you." Alexis shook her head. "Two weeks ago, I inherited a cattle ranch outside of Boulder. I had never set foot on a ranch in my life. I need someone to run the ranch, but my degree in management should allow me to do the books and take care of that sort of thing."

"How did you inherit a cattle ranch without ever stepping foot on one?"

"That's a good story for later," she whispered. She didn't want to color his opinion of her parents before he'd had a chance to have a meal with them.

"So where are we going for our bridal lunch?" he asked.

"There's a little Tex-Mex place not far from here. I want to try it to see if it's a place I can get Tex-Mex when the craving hits. I'm not sure how I'll survive otherwise."

"You're a fan of Tex-Mex?" he asked.

She nodded. "I've lived in Texas all my life, and I live and breathe for Tex-Mex. It's hard to believe people will eat inferior Mexican food when they can hold out for the best. If this place is as good as I hope it is, we'll be going there often."

Kyle smiled. "All right. Okay if we take my truck?" he asked.

"We'll have to. I rode in with my parents."

"Sounds good. Just let me know how to get there."

"I have it pulled up on my phone, and Siri will lead us there."

Chapter Three

At the restaurant, they joined Alexis's family in one corner where two tables had been pushed together. "Mom, Dad, this is Kyle. Kyle, my parents, my brother Brent, and my sister Brittany. They'll be going back to Texas this afternoon."

Kyle nodded. "It's nice to meet all of you." As soon as Alexis had taken her seat, Kyle took one beside her. He felt strange being at this little family gathering, with everyone knowing he was going to bed with Alexis.

Alexis was too busy with the menu to say anything else. "I'm going to keep it simple," she said. "Beef enchiladas with sour cream sauce and rice and beans. We're getting queso, right?"

"Of course," her mother said. "We're not animals."

She closed the menu and turned to Kyle. "What are you getting?"

He shrugged. "Probably just tacos. They've got bison tacos here. I've been working on a bison ranch since I finished school, and I've really grown to love bison meat."

"My ranch just has cattle."

"That's all right. I know lots about cattle as well." He took a chip and dipped it into the salsa. "Do you know that bison are the only cattle native to America? So, the rest of the cattle have been shipped in, and they have to go through a lot more inoculations than bison, because bison have natural resistances to things here."

"Interesting," she said. "Maybe we can have a few bison as well as the beef cattle. My current foreman, Joe Cahill, will be happy to talk about all that, but I've only got him for another five weeks before he retires."

"I see. I'll definitely be working closely with him then." He shook his head. "No one told me that I was going to be able to ranch when I married you."

"That's Dr. Lachele's fault," Alexis said. "I let her know I needed a cowboy to run my ranch on my first phone call with her."

"And it makes sense that she matched you with me then." He reached for her hand under the table and squeezed it. It felt different when he touched her now. At the church, it had just felt right when they touched. Now, she felt...attraction to him. His smile made her heart flutter.

Mom looked at Alexis. "You're going to have to keep in touch, and I don't mean like you did in college with just email. You will be calling at least twice a week, and hopefully Skyping."

Alexis nodded. "I know. But remember, Skype and phones work both ways. If it seems like it's been too long since we've talked, you should call me. I'll have a flexible schedule for the most part."

"How are you doing on days?" her dad asked. "I know you had a hard time every time you had to be on days for any period of time back in Texas."

She nodded. "I've been working on it slowly. Getting up earlier every day. Still not up with the chickens, but I'm up by nine most days."

Kyle looked at her oddly. "Nine? On a ranch, we're usually at work by six-thirty."

She smiled. "Three weeks ago, I was working in a call center from nine at night until six in the morning. I'm pretty proud that I've adjusted to nine. I'm still working on it, and soon I'll be up by five with the rest of you."

"That makes sense then."

She nodded. "At first, I'm probably going to hire a housekeeper. She can fix breakfast and keep the house clean while I sort through all the ranch's files and learn if anything has been neglected. I'm doing a major overhaul but it feels like I've done nothing."

Mom shook her head. "I can attest to the fact that you've worked your butt off." She looked at Kyle. "I've been staying with her for the past week to get everything ready for the wedding. We at least have the master bedroom ready for the two of you." Looking back at Alexis she frowned. "We forgot to take all of those clothes to the women's shelter in town."

"I'll take care of it this week," Alexis said. "It's not like we're driving three hours into town."

"How far out is the ranch?" Kyle asked.

"About twenty minutes," she said. "And I will be donating a lot. I may have to use the truck at the ranch."

"The ranch came with a truck?" he asked.

"Two of them actually. One for the owner and one for the foreman, who I won't have in five weeks, so we'll have plenty of trucks to go around."

"Sounds like you're making a lot of changes," he said.

"I need to. There is so much to be done, and I'm learning as I go."

Their food came then, and it looked as it should. She was very leery of eating Mexican food outside of Texas, though. She used her fork to poke at her enchiladas, before cutting off a bite and popping it into her mouth. When she finished chewing, she smiled happily. "It's good!"

The rest of her family had waited for her to announce it was good before they'd even tried their food. Kyle looked between them, uncertain what to think. "Why wouldn't it be good?"

Her dad answered that for them. "We're used to Tex-Mex, and it's a different taste than most Mexican food. We were hoping to find a restaurant that would serve good Tex-Mex for Alexis before leaving. She's all about Tacos and enchiladas. I swear the girl would swim in queso if given the chance."

Alexis could only nod her agreement. "And now we have a place, so we don't have to worry. When I'm craving Tex-Mex, we'll come here."

She took a bite of the refried beans and smiled. "The beans are good too."

They all talked and laughed while they ate, but Kyle noticed her brother Brent was quiet. He looked at him. "Not much to say?"

Brent shrugged. "My sisters have so much to say, that I rarely get a turn so I've learned to just wait."

Kyle laughed. "I'm an only child, but I spent a lot of time at my best friend's house growing up. He had two sisters, and they were obnoxious to deal with."

When they were finished, Alexis hugged her family goodbye. "I'll visit. I promise. But I want all of you to know you're welcome to come and visit us."

"I'm taking you up on that," Brittany said.

"You'd better!"

As they drove off, Alexis's heart sank a bit. She would miss her family, but she was happy to have their blessing before they left.

They got into Kyle's truck, and she gave him directions to the ranch. "So, just to explain what's happened here, I found out three weeks ago that my father is not my biological father. My bio dad and my mom split while she was pregnant with me, and he decided to give up parental rights so I wouldn't feel torn between the two of them. My stepdad adopted me when I was a year old, and together they had Brent and Brittany."

"And you never knew?"

She shook her head. "He paid for half of my college education, and he was always sending presents that my mom disguised by saying they were from a made-up great aunt. Mom stayed in touch with him, so he would always know what was happening with me, and she would send him pictures of me. He died and his lawyer contacted me about being there for the reading of the will. And now, three weeks later, I'm the owner of a ranch, knowing absolutely nothing about cows."

Kyle shook his head. "That's crazy."

"I know. And the ranch is huge. It's a massive piece of land with thousands upon thousands of cattle. At last count, we had fifteen thousand."

"That's a big enterprise. And you want me to run it?" Kyle was amazed.

"I know nothing about cattle," she reminded him.

"Then it's my job to run it. I'm really glad you've got a few weeks before your foreman is leaving. I've got a lot to learn."

"You really do. And I can't help much, but I do have a management degree that I can use to keep the books and make sure everything looks good on paper. It'll be your job to keep everyone working."

"I've never worked as a foreman. I was a cowboy for Scott Ward up in Montana, and I have been for over ten years, but that doesn't mean I know how to run a ranch." Kyle was very worried about letting her down.

"I think Joe will be able to teach you what you need to know. I'm not asking for perfection, you know."

He nodded. "I knew I was moving to Colorado, but I didn't know what I'd do here. I actually have an application in on your ranch to come in and work as a cowboy."

She laughed. "Well, you're getting the job, but it may be a little different than expected."

He pulled through the gate and over to park in front of the house. "I guess those Texas plates are yours?" he asked.

She nodded. "That's something I need to deal with soon. Getting Colorado plates. And everyone in Texas says Colorado wrong, and I feel like I mess it up all the time."

He chuckled. "Yeah, I've heard the same with Nevada. Very strange to me that they change the pronunciation of a state without permission." He winked at her.

She laughed, opening the door and getting down from the high seat of the truck. "I'm going to change into real clothes before I show you around, if that's all right."

"Just so you let me do the same, and I'll be as happy as a clam, though I don't know why everyone thinks clams are happy."

"I've always wondered that as well. I think we'll be good together."

He shook his head. "I thought I was getting a wife. I got a whole job as well."

She pushed the door open. "If you don't mind, I think I want to get to know you a little better before we have a wedding night, so I'm putting you in a bedroom across the hall from the master. Is that all right?"

He nodded. "I think that's a great idea. I don't know you well enough to make love with you tonight, and I'm dead tired."

She led him through the living room and down a hall beyond it. "I'm the last door on the left, and you're the last door on the right," she told him. "I'll change into me really quick, and we'll meet in the living room."

"Works for me."

Ten minutes later, they both emerged, her in shorts and a tank top and him in Wranglers and a button-down shirt. She smiled. "I feel like me again."

"Me too! That's a nice room you gave me."

"Mine's better," she said with a grin. "Separate bath and shower, and bath has a jacuzzi tub."

"Nice!" he said. "I assume I'll one day share that room with you."

"One day."

She gave him the full tour of the house, showing him all six bedrooms, the office, which she had taken over, the kitchen, with barstools up to the counter and a table, and then the formal dining room. "There's even another TV room upstairs. I don't know what my father called it, but that's what makes sense to me."

She took him out back, showing him the porch swing and the view of the mountains. "I love it here. My mom hated it when she moved here."

"How long was your mom here?"

"I didn't ask, but I got the impression it was under six months." She shook her head. "I don't think she gave her marriage much of a chance, but I do know she's very happy with my father you met today, Brad."

"What was your bio-dad's name?"

"Alexander Thomas Tobias, so I'm Alexis Thomasina. Isn't that awful?"

He chuckled. "I don't know that your name would win any beauty contests...I love the name Alexis, but Thomasina?"

"He'd already agreed to let Mom raise me alone with only some financial support, so she felt that she should give me a name that would show where I came from." She shrugged. "Sure could have done without the Thomasina."

He sat down on the porch swing and patted the spot between them. He was ready for that kiss that they'd skipped at the church. "Do we have plans for the rest of the day?" he asked.

She shook her head. "No, we're free to do as we want. I plan to make a simple supper in a few hours, but other than that, we can just vegetate. I need it because the last couple of weeks have been a whirlwind that I never thought I'd get out of."

He draped his arm over her shoulders, and she moved a bit closer to him, feeling comforted and protected by him. "I think it'll be nice to have an evening to just get to know each other."

"The only plan I made is for you to meet with Joe on Monday, and probably take a tour of the ranch. He wanted to make sure you could ride first."

Kyle laughed. "I've been riding longer than I've been walking."

She grinned. "I have a feeling that will make Joe very happy. He said after he retires, he'll still be available to consult with."

"Good." Kyle felt like he'd need extra time. "Now tell me about Alexis. What was she like three weeks ago before she inherited the biggest ranch I've ever seen."

"I was working in a call center, and they were talking about promoting me to a manager. I got my degree in management from the University of Texas at Arlington. I had a little apartment close to where I grew up, and I'd lived there for a few years."

"Wow," he said. "I didn't realize I was married to a college graduate."

She laughed at that. "And you're still more qualified to run this ranch than I am."

Kyle felt panicked every time she mentioned him running the ranch. Surely, he would need help with everything he did. "I hope I'm ready. What do you like to do in your spare time?" he asked.

She shrugged. "I love to read. I'm one of those weirdos who actually enjoys reading history texts just for fun. I also read business books for fun."

"Sounds like you're the life of the party."

She laughed. "Sure. Everyone wants to party with the girl with her nose in a book."

"I do," he said. "We didn't have our first kiss at the wedding. Not really. Is now too soon?"

She smiled, shaking her head. "Now would be wonderful."

He lowered his head to hers, and this time his lips didn't skirt away as soon as she felt them. No, he planted a real kiss on her mouth, and she wrapped her arms around him, enjoying it immensely. When he lifted his head, his eyes were a bit dazed. "You pack a wallop, Mrs. Stifter."

"As do you, Mr. Stifter."

He kissed her again, and this time she didn't want him to let go. They were married after all.

Chapter Four

They spent the day getting to know one another, with Kyle asking questions about the ranch Alexis simply couldn't answer. Finally, he asked if they could just go walk around, or even take his truck over the dirt roads that seemed to go everywhere.

"I'm not up to that kind of walk, but I'd be happy to drive and see what we see. I haven't even met most of the men yet because I've been working on the house."

"Most people don't take long walks around ranches on their wedding day," he said with a smile. "Put some shoes on though. Not flip flops. We may want to get out from time to time. Any idea how many acres this is?"

"I have no concept of what an acre even is, but I can find the information for you. Give me a second."

She came back wearing socks and shoes with the figure he'd asked for. "Looks like it's about three hundred seventy five thousand acres."

He gaped at her. "Do you have any idea how big that is?"

She shrugged. "Still no concept of an acre."

"That's almost six hundred square miles. I've never even imagined seeing a spread this big."

"Hey, I didn't know this place existed a month ago."

"I did. It's one of the ranches people talk about. And you guys raise purebred Angus beef. The good stuff."

"You guys? I hope you mean *we* are raising purebred Angus and not just me."

"Oh, yeah. That's what I meant." He grinned at her, taking her hand and pulling her toward the front door. "I'm feeling so much less sleepy with the thought of seeing the ranch."

She smiled, nodding emphatically. "I'm excited to see it too. I just haven't taken the time yet. As soon as I found out I was inheriting it, I drove out here to see the house, but not the ranch itself. My bio father wrote me a letter to tell me I should marry a cowboy who could manage it all for me, and I could do the books."

"It sounds like he really trusted you to make the most of this place."

She nodded, climbing into his truck. "I'm short," she said. "Any chance of getting a step installed for me over here?"

He chuckled. "If you can find someone to do it and take it in to have them install it while I'm out working one day."

"Ugh. I need to find someone who will take care of the lawn and a housekeeper. Like ASAP on both."

"Who did the lawn for your father?" he asked.

"I asked Joe that same question. He said my dad loved mowing so much he wouldn't let anyone else do it. He drove around on a riding mower, and just loved every minute of it."

Kyle sighed. "He sounds like he was a pretty special man."

She nodded. "And I never once met him. Not even when I was a baby. I almost feel cheated out of half of my heritage."

"Are you angry with your mother?" he asked.

She shook her head. "No, she didn't want me to feel like I was less loved than my siblings, which I get, but I wish I could have known him."

"I understand," he said, though he was unsure anyone could truly understand. He'd only heard wonderful things about the owner of Tobias Ranch, and here she was, his daughter, and she'd never heard a word about him until she was in her twenties, and he'd passed. "Okay. I'm just going to follow dirt roads, and we'll see where we land."

"I just hope we can find our way back when we're done."

He laughed. "You never know." They drove along roads for the next hour, pointing out portions of the herd when they saw them. "There's a stable?" he asked.

She nodded. "Close to the house. Barn as well. And chicken coop. I've taken over the feeding of the chickens, but that's about all I do for the animals around here. Maybe we need to get a kitten or two. My dad was always allergic so I never got one."

"I'm not allergic. Go for it, if that's what you want."

"Really?" she asked. She'd said it half-jokingly, but she did love animals. "You wouldn't mind?"

"Nah. And you're going into town to take all those clothes to charity anyway."

"True," she said. "I may just do that."

"Wouldn't bother me a lick."

Finally, they returned to the ranch, shortly before suppertime, and she hurried into the kitchen. "I got a frozen lasagna for tonight because I didn't want to have to cook. Can you wait a little while?" she asked.

"Of course," he said, happy to make her day easier.

They went into the living room and sat together on the couch. "You've heard all about my family today. Tell me about yours."

He shrugged. "For as long as I can remember, it was just me and my mom. My dad died when I was little, and she raised me alone."

"She never remarried?"

"Nope. She said there was no other man alive who could hold a candle to my father, so she was going to remain single for the rest of her life."

"Wow," she said. "Sounds like he was practically perfect in every way."

He chuckled. "I don't know about that. I have no memories of him, but there are a few photos of him putting me on horses. He was a rancher, but Mom wanted nothing to do with the ranch after he died, so she sold it."

"That's sad. You could have been running your own ranch for years now."

"I haven't felt ready. I'm still not sure if I'm ready. As much as I love ranching and working with cattle, there are so many things I don't know. I follow orders. I don't give them."

"I have faith in you," she said. "Dr. Lachele said you would be perfect for me."

"And you are perfect in my eyes," he said. "I'm impressed that you're not bitter toward your parents. I don't know that I could still feel so devoted to them after that."

She nodded. "But I had a wonderful childhood. And it sounds like it was my bio dad's decision to not have me go back and forth between them."

He looked around the room. "But he has almost a shrine to you in here. You're staring down at me from every wall."

"Just one of those things I haven't gotten around to changing yet. Once I've got a housekeeper hired, I can have her do projects like that with me."

"Have you put an ad anywhere?"

She nodded. "Yes, I actually found an online agency that will place domestic help anywhere in the US. I've got three interviews set up for Monday, and I'll do them all through Skype."

He nodded. "I think that's a pretty brilliant way to go about finding someone."

"I sure hope it works like I think it will."

"Me too. You don't need to spend a ton of time on that as you're getting the business part of the ranch figured out. I guess your dad did all of that himself?"

She nodded. "Yup. He has a CPA, but he just did taxes. This ranch has over three-hundred full-time employees. Maybe I should hire a couple more just to help out with the business side of things."

"You'd have to really trust your people," he said.

"I know. I'll think about that later. I don't know how Alexander did it. I don't even know what to call the man. Brad has been my father for as long as I can remember, and Alexander did so much for me without me knowing, and he's my father, but I have a dad."

"Call him Alex to me, and I'll know who you mean. Don't twist your brain into a knot trying to figure it all out."

When the timer for the lasagna went off, she jumped up. "I'm so hungry!"

"Me too!"

"Do you want to sit at the table in the kitchen or at the barstools? I don't care either way."

"Table then. I'd rather look at you while I eat than at the kitchen."

She laughed. "I would rather look at you."

She carried the lasagna tray to the table and set it down on hot pads she'd laid out after putting the lasagna in the oven. "If this isn't the best lasagna you've ever had, just remember I didn't make it."

He chuckled. "It's perfect because you weren't on your feet cooking for hours, and I still get fed."

"That's what I'm hoping for with a housekeeper. This place is huge, and if I was going to do all the cleaning and all the cooking, there would be no time left for me to run the business the way it needs to be run."

He nodded. "I agree. I hope you find someone quick."

"Me too. You won't mind a live-in, will you? I'd probably give her a room upstairs, and we'd keep ours down, so she wouldn't really get in our way."

"Oh, I think that's just fine," he said, forking a bite of the lasagna up and blowing on it. "It's good."

She smiled. "Good. If I'm in a hurry, I'll buy that brand again."

"Sounds smart."

"I'm really glad we have this weekend to get to know each other before we both have to hit the ground running on Monday."

He nodded. "Me too. And I need a couple of days to wrap my head around running a ranch this size."

"I'm a little overwhelmed with it myself."

"Once we have good people in place, it'll all seem easy."

"I sure hope so!" she said.

After supper, he helped with the few dishes, and they collapsed onto the couch again. "I don't know how much longer I can stay awake," he said.

She laughed. "I was just thinking the same thing."

Kyle gave her a crooked grin. "Would you hate me if I said goodnight now?"

Alexis shook her head. "I haven't slept in a couple of days," she said. "I drank a lot of coffee this morning, but it's long since worn off."

He stood up and reached down a hand to help her to her feet. "Bed then." He walked her down the hall, kissing her before they each went into their separate rooms.

Alexis thought about taking a long hot bath with a book, but then she realized that she had a good chance of falling asleep. No, it would be better if she collapsed and forgot the world.

She stripped down and put on a pair of pajamas she liked, then snuggled into the big bed. For a moment, she wished Kyle was there, but why have a wedding night if you would never be able to remember it, and may just fall asleep during it?

She was asleep as soon as her eyes closed, and she slept deep and dreamlessly.

She woke up at six the following morning, surprising herself. Finally, she'd had a decent night of sleep, since they'd been in bed by eight. She walked out into the kitchen and started to throw breakfast together, planning on French toast with bacon, one of her favorite meals from childhood.

She hadn't been up long when Kyle came out of his room, looking ready to take on the day. "I didn't expect you to be up so early!" he said.

She shrugged. "I finally had enough sleep last night. I hope you like bacon and French toast."

"Love it. Sounds like the perfect breakfast."

She took a sip out of the coffee she'd made. "Coffee?"

He nodded, walking over and helping himself to a cup. "Do we have plans for today?" he asked.

She shook her head. "We can do anything we want to do."

"Would you be willing to go into town with me?" he asked.

"Sure."

"I want to hit a Tractor Supply store and find a book on ranching. It may sound silly, but if I can get a better overall picture, instead of just knowing little pieces of it, I think I could do a better job."

She nodded, smiling. "Love that idea. Let's grab two of them. Then we could each have one to read."

"You're already shaping up to be a good wife."

"I sure do try," she said, grinning as she put bacon and French toast on two plates and carried them to the table. "Would you mind taking one of the ranch trucks?"

He shook his head. "You don't like mine?"

She laughed. "That's not it at all. One of them has steps to make it easier for me to get in!"

"How did I forget that you're a pocket-sized wife?"

As soon as they were finished eating, he helped her load the dishwasher, and then they headed into town. At the store, she saw a woman sitting outside with a bit of a scowl on her face. "Kittens?" the woman asked.

"Yes!" Alexis said. "Are they all from the same litter?"

The woman shook her head. "Two litters. This box has six-week-old kitties, and that has eight-week-old kitties."

Alexis reached into the box and picked up a pure white kitten with blue eyes. "Male or female?" she asked.

"Male."

From the other box, she grabbed a tortoise-colored kitten. "Male or female?" she asked.

"Female."

"I want them both. How much?"

The woman laughed. "They are free, and I'm happy to see you take them."

Alexis couldn't stop smiling. "What do they eat?"

"I have them on Purina Kitten Chow."

"We'll get some in the store. Thank you!" Alexis handed one of the kittens to Kyle who carried it with him, while she carried the other.

"I guess we're buying kitten supplies," he said, grinning at her. She looked as if she'd just gotten the most beautiful gift in the world.

"I don't even know what they need."

He chuckled. "I'll handle it."

They left the store thirty minutes later with a kitten carrier, food and water bowls, a scratching post and a litter box. And of course, the two books they'd gone for in the first place. They each found one that they liked better, and they were different books. "This way we can swap when we're done," she said.

He nodded. "We sure can. And hopefully, we'll each learn twice what we would have otherwise."

Chapter Five

Since the weekend was all the time they had for a honeymoon, they spent it reading and playing with the kittens. Alexis decided to call the white kitten Avalanche, which quickly got shortened to Lanche, and the Tortoise colored kitten, Tortie.

As soon as they got home, she set up their litter box and put out food and water bowls for them. They weren't super friendly with her yet, but she knew that would come with time as the kittens slid across the kitchen floor, slamming into cabinets and appliances.

Alexis looked at Kyle with wide eyes. "Will they always be this rambunctious?"

He chuckled, shaking his head. "They're kittens. They have extra energy. They'll be wrestling together and chasing each other around for a while, but then they'll settle down, and you will become a cat bed, which is pretty much the highest order of living when there's a cat around."

She giggled. "They're so much fun to watch!"

He nodded. "They are. And they've already figured out their litter box, which will make life a lot easier."

"Sounds like it." She yawned and stretched. "I want a nap, and I haven't even been up for very long."

He looked at her. "Don't do it. You're trying to get up earlier each morning, and that would mess you up terribly. As much as I love a nap, I realize they just aren't very good for me."

"I'll take your word for it." They were sitting on the couch together, so she rested her head on his shoulder for a moment. "If I don't get a nap, can we drive into town for supper? I don't think I'm up to cooking."

He nodded. "We can do that, but it'll be a lot harder to do during the week. We should get some groceries that we can put together fast. Well, that you can put together fast. I'm terrible at cooking."

"All right. Hopefully, we'll have a housekeeper soon, and she'll be in charge of cooking." She yawned behind her hand. "I hope the interviews go well. I looked up a list of questions to ask a potential housekeeper online. I think I have figured out how I'll handle things."

"I know you'll do great." He turned his attention back to his book, and she did the same.

When it was getting close to time to eat supper, she quickly pulled up a list of restaurants in the Boulder area with her phone. "We have many choices," she said. "Texas Roadhouse, Olive Garden, Chili's, Red Lobster...Any of those sound appealing? They're my favorite four from the list."

He tilted his head to one side and thought about it. "Let's do Roadhouse. I haven't had a good chicken-fried steak in forever."

"Sounds good to me. I wish I could take you to Babe's for chicken-fried steak, though. They are a staple in North Texas, and I went several times. It was always kind of special, and their chicken-fried steak is the best around...hands down."

"Maybe we can do that when we're visiting your family at some point."

She smiled. "I'm glad you're open to visiting my family. Give me a minute, and I'll be ready."

He settled comfortably on the couch, one leg taking over the spot where she'd been. Women never took a minute when they said a minute. At least that's what he'd always been told.

She came out a minute later. "You ready?"

"You weren't supposed to take a minute!" he said. "You said you'd take a minute, and that's supposed to be ten minutes in women's speak."

She smiled. "I'm sorry I'm not living down to your expectations."

He stood up, shaking his head. "Scott, the man I used to work for, would tell me all these things about women and how they never did what they said they'd do. I think he was just a chauvinist, though."

She smiled. "He sounds interesting."

"He is very interesting. He and his wife were the first couple matched by Dr. Lachele. He was clueless about women and took his frustrations with his wife out on his ranch hands, mostly me. He once told me I needed to have my mama buy me some clothes that wouldn't hurt his eyes."

She giggled. "Tell the truth now...did your mama buy your clothes?"

He shrugged. "I was still living at home at that point, and she did buy my clothes, but he didn't have to be so rude about it."

"What were you wearing?"

He sighed. "I was wearing Wranglers and a flannel shirt. But my mom kept getting creative with the flannel, and this one was purple with red. Truly hideous."

She laughed. "Sorry. I want to meet this guy now."

"Of course, you do. Not happening. Not anytime soon anyway." He shook his head. "The man was my boss for ten years, and I remember very few truly kind things he ever said."

"Why did you stay so long then?"

"Because I loved the work. I didn't feel ready to go anywhere else. I was happy there."

"Your mom didn't want to come to the wedding?"

"She said she reserved the right to come sometime in the next six months, where she could get to know you, and see how we were really getting along. A wedding wouldn't have allowed her to really get to know you."

"That's very true," she said. "My family is the type that will plan to come see us whenever they can fit it in. So be prepared for that to happen as well."

They got into his truck and drove to the Texas Roadhouse with the help of her phone's navigation system. "They don't look too horribly busy," she said.

"That's because they opened ten minutes ago," he said with a laugh. "The best thing about this place is they don't open til four in the evening."

After supper, they drove through Boulder, both of them trying to get their bearings. It was hard to figure out where everything was, but she spotted Walmart and Target. "Those are the stores I'll need most. Is it too much to ask of a housekeeper to grocery shop as well? Man, I would love to never shop again."

He laughed. "If it is too much to ask, then we'll just need to do the Walmart grocery pickup, and make our lives easier."

"Sounds like a plan."

It was shortly after six when they got home that evening, and they returned to the couch to continue reading. "I have about an hour before I want to head to bed," he said.

"I'll do the same," she said. "I really do want to live the same hours as a normal person."

"You're mostly normal. I like that about you."

She opened her book and read for a while, wanting to finish it that night, so she and Kyle could swap. He looked like he was nearing the end of his book as well. "Are you learning anything?" she asked.

"I think so. I'm getting a better idea of the business side of things at least."

"I'm learning more about the day-to-day operations. Maybe we each picked the wrong book."

He chuckled. "Sounds like we did."

She finished her book a few minutes before seven-thirty. When she looked over at him, he was finished and watching her. She held her book out and took his. "I may just have to read some tomorrow while you work."

He shrugged. "Now that we don't have to trade again, do whatever you need to do."

She stretched. "Bedtime, right?"

"Absolutely, but I need at least a goodnight kiss. And maybe a little goodnight groping."

She couldn't help but laugh at that. "Groping, huh?"

"Yup. It's time."

He pulled her toward him and kissed her, causing her knees to grow weak. Instead of remaining passive, she climbed onto his lap and kissed him back. When she felt his hand under her shirt, caressing the soft skin of her belly, she moaned softly into his mouth.

Kyle pulled back for a moment. "Why are we waiting again?"

"We want to know each other better."

"I already know a million times more about you than I did at this time yesterday."

"And you think that's enough?" she asked.

One of the kittens jumped on the sofa and then jumped right between them. He perched on Alexis's breasts. She couldn't help but giggle. "Do you want in on the action, Lanche?"

He looked at her curiously with his wide blue eyes, as if he was trying to figure out what they were doing.

Alexis moved off Kyle's lap and just held the kitten for a moment, glad there had been a distraction. She had a lot of feelings building for Kyle, but she wanted their marriage to be more about caring for each other than working and sleeping together.

"Where'd Tortie go? Huh? Aren't you two supposed to be playing together?"

Lanche leaped off her in response to her question, and he hurried down the hall to do something, but she was pretty sure she'd rather not know what.

"Saved by the kitten," he murmured.

She nodded. "Do you think they'll destroy the house while we sleep?"

"Nah. The scratching post should be enough to take care of the problem. They're rambunctious, but not destructive."

She stood. "I'm going to bed. Thank you for spending the day with me, and for letting me get kittens. Now that I have them, I feel a little guilty that we didn't rescue them."

"Don't. If you hadn't taken them, they'd have ended up in a shelter somewhere most likely. You did rescue them."

"Oh good!" They kissed once more outside their bedrooms, and Kyle sighed into her mouth.

"I hope this separate rooms thing doesn't last too terribly long. I'm ready to share."

She smiled. "Why don't we plan on a week? Then we'll know if we get along well and can handle being dead tired together."

He nodded, smiling. "Any idea where I'm supposed to go in the morning?" he asked.

"Joe said to have you meet him in front of the stable at six."

"Sounds perfect," he said, kissing her one last time before disappearing inside his room.

Alexis went into hers and closed the door, after contemplating for a moment if she should leave the door open for the kittens. She finally decided that it would be better if she just closed it.

She spent a few minutes getting ready for bed before climbing between the sheets. It still felt odd sleeping in someone else's bed at night, but it also made her feel a bit closer to her father. She hoped one day, she could understand him a bit better.

ALEXIS WOKE TO HER alarm at five the following morning and rubbed her eyes. Food. She had to fix breakfast for Kyle, and he had to be outside by six. She walked down the hall and quickly made one of her favorite breakfast meals. Eggs over medium with hashbrowns and bacon. Surely everyone loved a breakfast like that.

Kyle was there just as she was flipping the first of the eggs onto a plate for him that had already had bacon and hashbrowns added. He took the plate, kissed her quickly, and walked to the table. "Orange juice or coffee?" she asked.

"Both."

She nodded, using the Keurig for the coffee and getting the jug of juice from the fridge, pouring it into a small glass, and carrying it to the table. Then she fixed her own plate, and her own coffee, and joined him.

"I have my first interview at eight. Then one at ten, and one at two. Hopefully, by the end of the day, I'll have a decision made, and we can move forward past this."

"I'm just hoping this Joe person is planning on holding my hand through all of this and getting me ready to take over for him. I want to have the best beginning I can possibly have."

"If you have questions, could you call Scott?"

Kyle nodded. "I could. I'd rather not, but I could. I shouldn't say that. Scott is a nice guy. I just don't like how prickly he gets when he's tired."

"I can understand that," Alexis said. "Do you need more of anything?" He had just finished eating.

"No, that was good. Thank you. I'm going to put my plate in the sink and run some water over it, so it'll be easier to deal with when you're ready."

"Thank you!" Alexis liked that he thought of her when he did things. It felt right.

He leaned down and kissed her before heading for the door. "I'll be a little early, but I think that's good on my first day."

"Be careful!" she called after him. She was glad she had a little time before the first interview. She'd clean the kitchen and decide what to make for supper. She loved to use a crockpot, so she'd make sure to put everything in around noon.

Her first interview was with a woman who looked to be in her forties in New York. "I've been a housekeeper for an elderly gentleman here for many years. When he died last month, I knew I had to find a new position."

Alexis ran down the list of questions she'd prepared and finished with, "Do you have a driver's license? I would probably want to send you out for groceries."

The woman shook her head. "I do not. I would be happy to do the shopping, but I would need someone to drive me."

When Stephanie didn't suggest getting her own license, Alexis jotted that down. Everything else about her was perfect, and it sounded like she was willing to do just about anything that needed done around the house. "Oh, I almost forgot! Are you allergic to cats?"

"I'm not. I enjoy cats a great deal."

"Perfect. I'll let you know either way. I plan to make my decision today."

Stephanie nodded. "I appreciate the time you've given me."

As soon as she ended the call, Alexis made more extensive notes. She didn't want the people she interviewed later in the day to have an unfair advantage, simply because she wouldn't remember Stephanie's answers as well.

Between calls, she did a load of laundry, going into the room Kyle was using and grabbing his laundry as well. Thankfully, there was a laundry room just off the kitchen, so she wouldn't have to run up and downstairs to keep the laundry done up.

There was enough for two loads, and she could have them done that day. She would have to sit down and actually look at the business end of things soon, but she wanted everything else in place first.

The first load was in the dryer when she sat down to interview the second person, who was Rebekah and located in Wyoming, which was much closer. She started the call, and it was obvious Rebekah was waiting for her. "Rebekah?" she asked.

The other woman nodded. "Yes."

Rebekah looked to be in her late thirties. "It's good to meet you," Alexis said. "I'm Alexis, and I'm located in Boulder, Colorado. Would you be able to leave Wyoming and come here?"

Chapter Six

By the end of the day, it was clear that Alexis needed to hire Rebekah. The woman's only child had just gone off to college, and she was ready to move on as well. She had a driver's license, and she had agreed to all of the tasks Alexis had said would be hers.

When Alexis called just after five, she offered Rebekah the position, asking how soon she could start. "I've already packed everything up. I can drive your way tomorrow afternoon, if that's not too soon. I've arranged for my home here to be an Airbnb, and the first guests will be here Friday."

"Perfect timing then. Let me give you the address here..."

Supper was ready when Kyle walked in the door. She'd made a pork roast in the crockpot, complete with potatoes, onions, and carrots. She used the juices to make gravy for the potatoes, and popped some Pillsbury biscuits into the oven around ten minutes before she thought he'd be home.

As she got all the final touches together, she thought about how nice it would be once Rebekah arrived, and supper would no longer be her responsibility. She may even be able to talk Rebekah into making them suppers for her nights off. That would truly be wonderful.

Kyle got in shortly after six-thirty, and she put supper on the table immediately. "How was the first day?"

He walked into the kitchen and washed his hands. "Busy. Joe is actually teaching me this week, and next week he wants me to take over with him shadowing me. It's going to be a long five weeks."

"But did you like the work?"

"Of course, I did," he said.

Alexis smiled. "Good. I was worried that I'd married a man who would hate that type of work."

"It's really not that much different from what I was doing, I just have to lead the others, which means I need to know what needs to be done each day, which I'm learning from Joe. He talks about your father all the time. He seems to think Alex knew everything in the world about ranching, and no one will ever be able to fill his cowboy boots."

She smiled, nodding. "I got the same impression from him while we talked."

"This operation is massive. I knew that in one part of my mind, but in another, I'm learning a lot myself. King Ranch in Texas is the largest cattle ranch in the US. We're about half the size of King Ranch, but so much bigger than any I've been involved with. Joe said I'll be able to call him to consult any time, so that's going to help a lot too."

She sat down across from him, nodding. "Sounds like there's a lot to learn."

"He did tell me that there were certain people who worked here that helped with the books. There's a whole team of them, and they will be here when you need them. They work part-time on the books and part-time with the cattle. They'll have a good knowledge of everything that needs to happen."

"Ask Joe to have them come in on Friday, so I can pick their brains." Alexis shook her head. "I feel like I'm lost at sea still."

"I'm right there with you," he said.

She squealed jumping up. "One of the kittens just attacked my foot."

He chuckled. "That's just part of having critters, I think."

"I'm sure it is. Just scared me for a second."

"How did your calls go with the housekeepers?" he asked.

"Really well. I could have been happy with any of the three, but I think the best fit for us is a former high school janitor from Wyoming.

Her name is Rebekah, and she's going to start driving in the morning. I expect her to be here by tomorrow evening from what she said."

"Oh, that's fabulous. Why her and not one of the others?"

"The first one couldn't drive. I talked to Rebekah second, and she just seemed to fit. Then the third one was more of a nanny than a housekeeper, and though I do hope we'll have children before too terribly long, I want the focus on the house and not children."

"Makes sense. Now you won't have to grocery shop," he said with a grin.

"And I do hate grocery shopping," she said. "At least for the first month, I'll make up menus for every night, but after that, I hope she can pretty much wing it. Which means, I need a list of all your favorite foods and one of the things you absolutely will not eat. Then I can turn that into a monthly menu for Rebekah."

"Sounds good to me," he said. "I can do that after supper. When are you planning to make up your menu?"

"Probably tonight after supper," she said. "Well, after dishes. I'll get them done while you make your lists, and then I'll work on the menu this evening."

"I think that's good. You're not expecting her to work tomorrow, are you?"

Alexis shook her head. "No, she'll probably not start til Wednesday or Thursday, so I'll plan on keeping up with everything until then." She took a sip of her water. "Oh! I almost forgot to tell you. I went into your room today to get your dirty clothes, and everything has been folded and placed on the foot of your bed."

"Thank you for doing that. I figured I'd do my own laundry."

"Not with the hours you'll be putting in on the ranch. You put in a twelve-hour day today."

"I had a thirty-minute lunch with the other men. There's a cook that deals with meals for the men in the bunkhouses, and he makes a big meal at lunch time as well. It was good not to have to worry about coming home for something."

"I didn't even know there was a cook! I can't wait to meet the people who do the books. I don't even know if the men have been paid since Alex died."

He smiled. "I did think of that and asked Joe. He said that they've all been paid on-time. Your father was never the one who dealt with payroll."

"Thank God," she said softly. "I'm just glad things are still running as smoothly as they can."

Her phone rang then, and she frowned. "I feel like I need to answer it."

"Go. You're not hurting my feelings."

Alexis stood and walked to the phone. "Hello?"

"Alexis?"

"Yes."

"This is Rebekah. I took a nap after we talked, and I'm going to go ahead and head down tonight. Is that a problem?"

"No, that makes me happy. I'll make sure your room is ready for you. I'm sure you'll get here after we're asleep, but there's a key under the turtle on the front porch. When you get in, you'll walk through the living room and then the kitchen. There's a set of stairs off the kitchen. Go up, and choose whichever room suits you best. I truly don't care which one you choose."

"That sounds easy enough. I'll meet you tomorrow then."

"Sounds perfect. Thanks for letting me know."

Kyle gave Alexis a confused look. "Is she coming later than she thought?"

Alexis shook her head. "She's leaving now. She'll get in while we're asleep tonight, and then we can talk through everything tomorrow."

"Oh, that's great. One day earlier is not something you could complain about in any way."

"I agree." She rubbed the back of her neck. "Everything seems to finally be falling into place."

"You look tense."

She nodded. "I've just had a lot on my shoulders since I got the call Alex died. I was shocked to find out what he'd left me."

"I'll rub your shoulders after making my list."

She smiled. "I would love that more than I can express."

While she did the dishes, he sat at the table with pen and paper and made two lists. When he handed her the paper, she glanced down at it. "Looks like we're pretty compatible food-wise. I can't stand pickles either. Why would anyone ruin a good burger with pickles?"

"My mom put relish in everything. I thought I hated potato salad until we had a big company picnic and Scott's wife, Savannah made hers. It was delicious. Everything is the same except for the pickles my mom puts in hers. They're so gross."

"And they take up more than their fair share of food space. I mean, you put them on a burger, and the whole bun is soaked in pickle pee."

He nodded. "I think pickles should be outlawed."

"Me too! I'm writing my congressman as soon as I figure out who that is!"

He chuckled. "It's like we've just moved here or something."

"Isn't it?"

She sat down on the couch with pen and paper in hand, wanting to incorporate his favorite things as well as her own into the menu she was making. She only hoped that Rebekah wouldn't mind cooking off her menu.

She tried to arrange simpler meals on the weekends that would reheat well. Then she would have a choice of cooking or she could grab something already made from the fridge.

As she was writing, one of the kittens jumped up on the couch and laid down across her notebook, rolling over to her back. "Tortie, what are you doing? Do you not want your mama to work?" Scratching the kitten's belly seemed to be a mistake when the kitten wrapped all four legs around her arm and bit her hand.

Kyle glanced over and laughed. "She's a menace."

"I can tell. I didn't give her permission to do that!"

Lanche climbed up his legs and jumped from Kyle's lap right onto Tortie, and the two kitties fell onto the floor in one heap. "Are they hurt?" Alexis asked.

Kyle shook his head. "No, they're playing. That's how kittens act."

"I guess I've only ever been around adult cats."

"Kittens are learning to be predators. They will stalk and kill prey, so they like to think they're little predators now as they attack each other."

She giggled. "We have two tiny little ferocious predators. I hope they don't have trouble killing their food!"

He smiled, stealing a quick kiss. "How long do you think the menu will take?"

"Just for the menu, probably an hour. But then I'll want to put a Walmart grocery order in and that part will take longer."

"Does it all have to be done tonight?" he asked.

"Absolutely not," she replied. "I want it done before the end of the day tomorrow."

"So there's time for a little kissing and petting tonight?"

"You want to kiss and pet our babies?" she asked. "You don't have to ask me. The pets belong to both of us."

He shook his head at her, noting the twinkle in her eyes. "I suppose you could look at it that way, but I really don't know why you would."

She laughed. "We'll have time."

"Good. Will we have time for me to carry you to my room and have my way with you?"

She shrugged. "I have no idea how long that takes."

"We could do a practice run and time it. For scientific purposes of course."

"Of course," she said with a grin. "I have to do this menu first, though."

He sighed. "I feel thwarted!"

"You should," she said softly. "I'm doing all I can to thwart you at every opportunity!"

"Well, you should stop that!" he protested. "I like the idea of having a sweet pliable wife who enjoys every second with me."

"What should we eat for supper on the seventeenth?" she asked, simply to get him to stop talking about sex.

"That sounds like a good night for beanie weenies."

"Sorry, you must have forgotten to put them on your list," Alexis said.

Kyle sighed. "You ask for my input, and then you argue with my answer! Is this what marriage to you will be like?"

"Oh, I think you'll find there are perks as well," she said.

"Like?"

She carefully set the notebook and pen on the coffee table and turned fully toward him on the couch. Her hands started at his waist as she carefully pushed his shirt up to his shoulders, her fingers tracing every inch of him. When she raised her lips to his, he immediately took over the kiss, but allowed her hands to keep exploring.

When she finally pulled away, she looked straight into his eyes. "Like that."

"You're killing me. Let's go to bed."

She tilted her head to one side for a moment before slowly nodding her agreement. He wasn't going to be able to think of anything else until they'd made love. That much was clear.

He stood and hoisted her up into his arms carrying her into her bedroom, putting her down on her feet right beside the bed. He quickly divested her of her shorts and t-shirt and threw his shirt onto the floor.

She sighed, shaking her head. "Now I'm just going to have to wash more dirty clothes."

He chuckled as he leaned down and kissed her again. Finally getting the go-ahead from her was like Christmas, her birthday, and Easter all rolled into one. He was like a kid with a brand-new toy that he couldn't wait to try out, but he was being careful with it, because he was afraid he'd break it.

Finally, he removed her bra and panties and pushed her down onto the bed, pushing down his jeans and underwear and moving down beside her. Cupping her face in his hands, he focused on simply kissing her. When her hands started stroking his body, he knew she was ready for more.

He touched her all over, his fingers and tongue, touching every inch of her body that was accessible to him.

When he finally moved to join their bodies together, Alexis was ready. She wanted Kyle in a way she'd never wanted a man in her life, and when he started to press into her, she gasped, surprised that it both hurt and felt so right all at once. How did anyone do this more than once, when surely they would have to spontaneously combust the first time.

Finally, when he was seated deeply inside her, he began moving, slow strokes while he watched her face intently, careful not to hurt her any more than he had to.

She was gasping for air, wanting to push him away and pull him to her all at once. Finally, he said, "Relax, and it'll happen."

So she wrapped her arms and legs around him, and did as he said. As soon as she'd stopped thinking about what she was supposed to be doing, she felt her climax build within her, and she let out a gasp of shock as she finished before him, lifting him off the bed with the force of her feelings.

He finished himself and moved beside her, out of breath but oh so relaxed. Finally.

Chapter Seven

Afterward, she snuggled up to him, and they both fell asleep. Alexis was so tired from having to change her schedule, and Kyle was just as tired after twelve hours of work.

When she woke in the morning, she realized she hadn't set her alarm, but there was something buzzing on the floor. Rolling out of bed, she walked around and grabbed his phone from the pocket of his jeans. "Shut your alarm off," she said, dropping the phone onto his chest as she headed into the bathroom to shower and get ready for her day.

She made the shower quick so she could get breakfast started, but when she walked into the kitchen, she was surprised to see Rebekah already there with breakfast ready.

She'd made some sort of breakfast casserole that Alexis was ready to dig into immediately. "You're my hero!" she said as she hurried into the kitchen and made a cup of coffee with the Keurig. "I figured you'd sleep til at least noon."

Rebekah laughed. "When you've gotten up at six in the morning for twenty years, it's not so easy to sleep until noon." She added a huge spoonful of the casserole to a plate and handed it to Alexis.

Alexis took a bite and smiled. "You weren't kidding about being able to cook, were you?"

Kyle joined them then, already dressed for his day. "You must be Rebekah."

"I am. It's good to meet you."

"I'm Kyle," he said, not wanting to stand on any kind of formalities.

She put food on a plate for him. "Do you want coffee?"

"Yes, please. And orange juice."

Rebekah had the drinks on the table in front of him in moments. "I hope you both like breakfast casserole because it's my favorite thing to eat in the mornings."

Alexis nodded, smiling. "This is really good. But my favorite thing about it is I didn't have to get up early to fix it."

Kyle nodded. "Very good. Eat with us!"

Rebekah shook her head. "I have too much coffee buzzing through my system to be able to sit."

"I started making a menu for the month for you, but I got distracted," Alexis said. She couldn't meet Kyle's gaze because she knew she would blush, and exactly what had distracted her would be obvious.

"We can work on it together today, if you want," Rebekah said.

"We need groceries badly," Alexis said. "We'll get the menu ready, and then I'll do an online order from Walmart. We can go get them together and we'll talk along the way so you know exactly what we need from you." Alexis hid a yawn behind her hand. "I was working an overnight shift until three weeks ago, and getting used to being up earlier than I ever went to bed may just be the end of me."

Rebekah laughed. "A leopard doesn't change his spots either. I can handle breakfast for Kyle if you want to sleep in later."

Alexis shook her head. "I've done it two days in a row now. It'll start getting easier any day. I'm sure of it."

Rebekah ate her share of the casserole standing up, and Alexis couldn't help but grin. "Do you always have so much energy?" she asked.

"Only when I drink a pot of coffee when I wake up," Rebekah responded.

After breakfast, Kyle kissed Alexis goodbye before going out to meet Joe at the stables again. It was becoming his routine, and he was just glad to have someone helping.

"I am so glad you're here!" Alexis said. "I know I just hired you yesterday, but I'm trying to keep up with household chores, cooking, learning the books for the ranch, and take care of two very ferocious little predators."

Rebekah laughed. "When I came in, I saw them, but they ran off as quickly as they could. The little white one is adorable. He's so fluffy!"

Alexis smiled. "He's long-haired. From what I understand, my father didn't want cats around, so there's a bit of a mouse problem. I decided to get two kittens from different litters so they could multiply and deal with the barn issues as well as keep me company. We just got them Sunday, so they're not exactly allowed outside yet."

"They'll need about two weeks of being just inside before they'll know where to come home to," Rebekah agreed.

"I kind of made a cleaning chart for myself for when I thought I was going to have to wait a bit for a housekeeper, but you can use it if you want."

"Are you one of those highly organized people who expects everything to be perfect all the time?"

Alexis laughed. "Not at all. But I attempt to be one of those highly organized people. I'm constantly making charts and lists and never accomplishing what's on them."

"It'll give me a place to start," Rebekah said smiling.

"I do keep a list of things we seem to be out of on a notepad on the fridge. Everything was perfectly organized when I arrived, and I'm just trying to keep it that way."

"We'll develop our own system as time goes by."

Alexis nodded, standing up to take her plate to the sink. "I got that. You work on your menu."

"Since we're newlyweds, I got Kyle to write me a list of his favorite meals and another of the things he simply refuses to eat. I'm using that as a jumping-off point for the menus."

Rebekah nodded. "Sounds smart."

Alexis worked on the menu for a while and when she had a full month's worth of meals, she gave it to Rebekah. "I've only done suppers. Kyle will eat most lunches with the men, and we're both wide open on what we'll eat for breakfast."

"I'll handle breakfast then," Rebekah said. "Is this the only refrigerator?"

Alexis shrugged. "There's a basement I haven't been in yet, and I have yet to wander out into the garage." She rubbed her hands over her face. "Three weeks ago, I received a call telling me my father was dead. It turns out that the father I've always known adopted me when I was a year old, and this house and ranch belonged to my biological father. He left everything to me."

"No wonder you don't know everything. You go check the garage, and I'll check the basement."

"Sounds good." Alexis found the door leading to the garage after looking for a bit, and she went out. There were both a refrigerator and a deep freeze out there. The freezer was stocked with frozen meals, all straight from the frozen food aisle. There were a couple of bags that were labeled chili that she was going to try when she had a moment.

Going back into the house, she saw Rebekah standing there. "There's a refrigerator and a deep freezer in the garage."

Rebekah nodded. "There are commercial laundry machines downstairs, but no refrigeration. I guess those were used for washing bedding. I don't know how long it's been since bedding has been washed, so I'm going to do the whole house this week."

"And you found a room to your liking?"

"Yes, I chose the first one I found, but it's a nice room. Full bath attached, and a flat screen tv mounted on one wall. I see that as something that will keep me happy for a very long time."

"Remind me to write the wi-fi password down for you later."

Rebekah nodded. "I'll need it. I'm addicted to all those silly games you can play on your phone."

"What else do I need to do to help you settle in before we get down to work?"

"Nothing that I can think of."

Alexis nodded. "Good. Basically, what I want from you are two meals a day. The outside freezer is filled with frozen meals that I'll nuke for myself for lunches. Keep everything up around the house. If we need to hire someone to come in and fix the plumbing or anything like that, I'll call someone, but you have to let me know when I need to. Since Kyle and I just moved here, we won't be having parties or anything. It's just keeping up with the house, and with only two of us to clean up after, it should be easy work."

"If I have time during my workday, is it all right if I get on my laptop?"

"Oh, absolutely. More games?"

Rebekah laughed. "Actually, I'm fulfilling a lifetime goal and writing a book. It's my first, and I'm sure it will be utter trash, but I promised myself, and I'm doing it."

"I think that's great!" Alexis said. "I always wanted to be a writer, but I don't have the talent, so I just read what other people write."

"I don't think I have the talent either. I guess we won't know until it's done." Rebekah glanced down at the menu for the month. "There are a few things on here that I may need recipes for."

"That's fine," Alexis said. "I used a lot of crockpot recipes, but you can do them however you want. Just know upfront that Kyle and I both despise pickles, and we'd rather not have it as part of our meals."

"Not even in potato salad?"

"Especially not in potato salad," Alexis said with a smile.

"All right."

"Now, I'm going to make a list of everything we need from Walmart, and you and I can go in for the grocery pickup together. I may even take you out to eat at the Tex-Mex place I found. I was born and raised in Texas, and I already miss Tex-Mex so much!"

"Then we'll go. It'll help me understand how you like your meals better anyway."

"What school is your son going to?" Alexis asked as she started writing down groceries they needed to buy based on the list she'd made.

"Harvard," Rebekah said, and Alexis could see the true pride on her face.

"Oh, that's wonderful!"

"He got a full ride. It's crazy to me to think that my baby is going to a school as prestigious as Harvard, and I don't have to pay a dime. Even his books are covered, and that's almost unheard of."

"You must be really proud of him."

"Oh, I definitely am. He wants to go into law, and his debate is what put him over the top. I mean, his 4.0 GPA didn't hurt, but it was his debate that got him the scholarship."

"What does he think of you moving away from his hometown?"

"He told me it was time," Rebekah said. "His father was worthless, and I couldn't seem to totally let him go while we lived in the same town. I'm sure this change is exactly what I need in life."

"Sounds like he wants only the best for his mom."

"He's an incredible kid. I can't deny it." Rebekah shook her head. "Now, we need to switch topics or I'll either spend the whole day crying because I miss him, or I'll talk about him so much, that you'll be looking for anything you can find to stick in your ears to block out the sound of my voice."

Alexis laughed. "I hope to have a child I can be that proud of one day."

While Alexis finished up her grocery list and got everything ordered, Rebekah cleaned the kitchen. And she didn't just give the counters a quick scrub, but she cleaned the front of the refrigerator, the stoves, and the other appliances. Then she mopped the floor in there.

"I cannot stand a dirty kitchen," Rebekah said as she was done.

"Well, I don't think you missed even a tiny speck of dirt, so it's all good," Alexis said.

"I got a pickup time between one and two. We should leave around noon, have lunch, and then head to Walmart."

"Sounds good to me," Rebekah said. "Am I allowed to clean cars as well?"

Alexis laughed. "Kyle drove down from Montana just a few days ago, and I drove from Texas not long before that. There are cars that must be cleaned."

"Oh, good. I like doing cars, because I can start with something filthy and have it perfectly clean within an hour or two."

"Sounds good to me. I need to spend some time this afternoon finding a lawn care guy. Apparently, Alex, my father took care of it himself, and I don't think that's something I want to do. We do have a nice riding mower in the garage though."

"I'm not great at lawns," Rebekah said. "I'd hire someone from town. Or let the cattle mow it."

Alexis laughed. "I can just imagine all the men's reactions if I let the cattle run around on the lawn to 'mow' it for me."

"Ahh...we don't care what the men think, do we?"

"We shouldn't..." Alexis walked back toward her bedroom. "I need to move all of Kyle's things into my room from the spare today too."

"You haven't been sleeping with your husband?" Rebekah asked, surprised.

"We were introduced at the altar on Saturday. We waited a couple of days to get to know one another."

"I love to read the old mail-order bride stories. Your marriage sounds like one of them."

Alexis nodded. "I'll be right back." Slipping into her room, she used the facilities and brushed her hair.

Rebekah was waiting for her in the living room. "I'll help you move his things this afternoon. I think in the beginning there will be lots of little projects."

"Yes! Like getting my pictures off the walls in the living room. I feel like I'm judging myself all the time."

"Were those there when you got here?"

Alexis nodded. "Apparently my father kept up with my life despite the fact that I had no idea who he was."

"That's crazy," Rebekah said.

"He even paid for half of my college tuition, and I'd never heard his name before." Alexis sighed. "It was the lawyer's idea for me to contact the woman who introduced Kyle and me. He and my father thought it would be a good idea for me to find a cowboy who could handle the day-to-day management of the ranch, while I worked on the business end of things."

"Sounds like your father was a very smart man!"

"I like to think so. I just wish I could have met him."

Chapter Eight

When Kyle walked in the door that evening, the house was filled with the delicious aroma of Italian cuisine. "Whatever that is, I sure hope it's done!" He leaned down and kissed Alexis, not touching her anywhere but her lips.

"It's frozen chicken ravioli, and alfredo sauce, along with garlic bread. Doesn't it smell amazing?"

"Yes!" He walked into the kitchen and washed his hands. "What a day!"

"What happened?" Alexis asked.

He sighed. "One of the fences got cut and we had a few hundred head of cattle in the neighbor's field. It took all afternoon to get them back. That's one thing that's the same between cattle and bison. Getting them back into the right enclosure is a pain in the butt."

"I'm sorry," Alexis said. "I found a lawn care guy today. I finished the menu for the month, and Rebekah and I went to town for groceries."

He nodded. "Sounds good. Looks like we're all getting a ton done around here."

"Oh, and Rebekah and I moved all your things into my room."

Kyle grinned. "That sounds like the most productive use of your time all day."

"I thought so," Alexis said, getting up from the couch and going into the kitchen. "Can I help you put anything on the table?"

"Just get drinks for the two of you, and I'll handle the rest," Rebekah said.

"Coke?" Alexis asked Kyle over her shoulder.

"Sounds good."

She grabbed herself a Barq's root beer and poured both drinks into glasses, carrying them to the table. She sat down with Kyle. "It was a busy day, and I still haven't started on the books."

"I would put that off until the other business people report for duty on Friday," Kyle said. "I talked to Joe about it today, and he said everyone gets paid on Saturday afternoons. The checks are cut on Fridays, and I'll take them with me when I go out and make sure everything is still going as it should on Saturday. Basically, means I'll ride around on Saturday afternoons to make sure all is good, and pass out checks while I'm there. It'll help me get to know the different people. Joe usually does it, but he wants me to start learning names."

Alexis nodded. "Maybe by next Friday, I'll know how to cut the checks myself." She looked at Rebekah. "Do you mind if we pay you on Friday afternoons after we cut the checks for the whole ranch?"

"Not at all. I think that's smart."

Alexis looked at Kyle. "Her son got a full-ride scholarship to Harvard!"

"That's amazing!"

"Especially considering his mama got married right out of high school and never even went to a day of college," Rebekah said, smiling. "I'm pretty proud of him."

"I would be too."

Rebekah carried their plates to them, setting them on the table in front of each of them. She put a basket full of garlic bread there as well.

"Are you going to eat with us?" Alexis asked.

"No, I'm going to go eat in my room and talk to my son. He's been texting that he has something exciting to tell me."

"Enjoy," Alexis said.

"I'll be out to do the dishes in a little while. Don't touch them!" Rebekah said.

"She's bossy," Kyle said as he watched her walk away.

"She's just trying to keep me from overextending myself," Alexis said.

He took a bite of his food and smiled. "This is absolutely amazing."

"I think so too. She used my recipe for the alfredo sauce, but she makes it better than I do. I'm impressed so far."

"I am too. Think she'll stick around?"

"I really do. She doesn't seem like the type of person to flit from one job to another."

Kyle nodded. "Joe is giving me a run for my money. He's over sixty, and he's outriding me. I thought I was good on a horse, but that man can do things I've never even dreamed of. He actually roped two calves at once today."

"Sounds amazing," Alexis said. "It sounds like he's the mentor you need as you learn the ropes."

"He definitely is," Kyle said. "I am learning so much every day. You should go with me when I ride out and give everyone their checks on Saturday."

She slowly shook her head. "I don't know how to ride."

"What? You grew up in Texas and you can't ride?"

"I grew up in the city," she explained. "I'd love to learn to ride, but I don't think I'll know what I'm doing well enough to go out with you on Saturday."

"I guess not," he said. "I'll teach you."

"Let's both figure out our jobs first. Maybe you can teach me in the spring."

He nodded. "Spring is so busy for ranchers. That's when all the cows drop their calves, and when we have to round up the calves to separate the bulls from the steers."

"What's the difference?" she asked.

He grinned. "A steer is a bull that's been castrated. Steers go to market, but we keep the bulls for breeding purposes."

"Oh. There's not a vet who castrates the steers?"

He shook his head. "No, most ranchers do it themselves. And they have a big party as part of it. We'll get neighbors to come and help, and we'll put on a big shindig with food and dancing. Trust me. It's an experience you'll never forget."

"All right. I'll make sure to look forward to that."

"Good girl," he said, pushing away his empty plate. "I could eat that for every meal."

She laughed. "I could too, but then I'd be bigger than one of your bulls."

Kyle shook his head. "One of our bulls, sweetheart."

BY THE END OF THE SUMMER, they both felt comfortable with their jobs. Alexis spent most of the day at a computer inside the house, while Kyle worked twelve-hour days.

At the end of October, his mother came for a visit, and she was a joy to be around. In Alexis's head, she was just like Rebekah, but when she met the woman, she knew better.

His mother, Joyce, chose to stay on the other side of the house with Rebekah rather than risk hearing anything coming from their bedroom. Alexis knew that was the reason because Joyce told her. "I'd rather sleep as far away from you and Kyle as possible. I do not need to hear the two of you enjoying each other."

Alexis had blushed. "We are married."

"I'm fully aware. Doesn't mean I want to hear anything I could possibly hear."

Alexis quickly changed the subject. "I don't know if you ride, but you're welcome to go out with Kyle or you can stay inside with me. I'll be doing payroll today, and that will take me all afternoon."

Joyce shrugged. "I may just spend my time in the kitchen with the lovely Rebekah. I enjoy cooking. I guess she could even take the day off if she wanted to."

When Alexis asked Rebekah what she wanted to do, she said she'd stay and do her job. "I don't like the idea of taking off with no notice, even if you do offer me the opportunity. But perhaps Joyce and I could cook together. The company makes everything more fun."

Kyle smiled at Alexis. He knew his mother was a bit pushy, and he hoped she and Alexis would get along well.

Kyle slipped out the door for his day of work, while Alexis went into the office her father had used. She booted up his computer and immediately went through all of the timecards, making sure each one was there before she started typing in the amounts of the checks.

At lunchtime, Joyce and Rebekah came to the study. "How much longer before you're ready for lunch?" Rebekah asked.

Alexis usually worked through her lunch hour, so she was a bit surprised by the question. "I can take a break anytime," she said.

"Good," Joyce said. "Come on."

The ladies had made a chicken alfredo pizza with bacon bits, and it was just coming out of the oven. "I was hoping we timed it well," Rebekah said.

"I can take off anytime," Alexis said, which was true. It was hard for her on Fridays to get all her work done, but she would make an exception this week while Joyce was visiting.

The three of them sat at the table, and talked, laughing often. It was just over an hour later when Alexis realized how long she'd been away from her desk. "I have to get back or everyone will not be getting a check tomorrow, and I have a feeling that the men would be unhappy about that."

Joyce nodded. "I don't know why they think they need to be paid for riding around on a horse all day and taking care of cattle. Kyle told me that after his first day working at Scott's ranch. But he sure was ready for his paycheck when it came."

Alexis nodded. "Sounds like Kyle." She hurried off and worked as quickly as she could for the rest of the day, getting her tasks done just as Kyle came in at the end of his day.

"I left the pile of paychecks on the corner of the desk in the office."

He nodded. "Did they distract you?"

She nodded. "I took an hour lunch, and I do take lunch some days, but never on Friday. But it was fun."

He nodded, understanding exactly how she felt. She wasn't one to have fun when there was work to be done. "She goes home Monday morning," he reminded her.

"I know. I'm truly enjoying her company, but I feel like I'm having to work at double speed to get everything done as I should."

"Makes sense," he said.

Supper that night was off-menu completely, but it was delicious, and Rebekah agreed to join them for a change.

"What is this?" Kyle asked after stirring the meal with his fork.

"Thai curry," Joyce told him. "I've been experimenting with it, and I think I got it just perfect."

"It's good," he said, still more toying with it than anything else.

"You need to open your mind to other culture's cuisines," his mother said. "I had this in a Thai restaurant not too terribly long ago, and I loved it so much, I just had to learn to make it."

"I really like it," Alexis said.

"Good. I'll leave the recipe with Rebekah, and she can make it for you then."

Alexis knew she'd need to make something for Kyle after the other women were asleep. She had kept up a supply of frozen meals for occasions just like this.

The women thankfully went to bed early, and she found something more to his liking in her stockpile of foods. "Do you think one meatloaf with mashed potatoes will be enough or should I make two?"

Kyle stood and watched her from the door to the garage. "I think I'll need two."

She hurried inside and put one in the microwave, planning on him working on that one while she cooked the second. "I didn't realize they switched the menu until after you got here. I'm sorry!"

He shrugged. "My mom kind of changes everything whenever I see her. I should have expected it, but I hoped she respected you enough not to do something like that in your home."

"It didn't matter to me. I enjoyed it."

"Mattered to me," he said, taking the first tray of meatloaf to the table and sitting down with it. "Does your mom do things like that?"

Alexis shook her head. "She never has. I think she knows that I do things differently than she does, and she doesn't mind at all. She thinks I should do things my own way."

"Good mother."

"I think it's different when you have a son," Alexis said. "You don't expect him to find new ways to do things, and you want his wife to do things the way you always did."

"Whatever the reason, I didn't like it," Kyle said. "We should have stuck with the menu you spent so much time preparing."

"Tomorrow, I'll tell them we're going to the Tex-Mex place. Then they can stay and cook for each other or eat what we want to eat."

Kyle smiled, nodding. "I love that little Tex-Mex place as much as you do."

When they went to bed that night, they were in good moods, despite the fact that he hadn't enjoyed supper. "I'm glad I finally got to meet your mother, but I hope she doesn't visit terribly often," Alexis said. "For you, and not for me. I've gotten along with her just fine."

He sighed. "I hope she doesn't visit terribly often either. She seems to really want to change everything around her whenever she visits me. I should have warned you."

"It's fine by me," she said, snuggling close to him. "I am sorry you didn't like supper though."

"Me too. It just wasn't my thing."

She kissed him, and he was soon distracted, thinking of nothing but her. They made love, and snuggled together when it was over. "I want to invite my family for Christmas," she said, after they'd laid there in silence for a while.

He nodded. "Probably best to talk to me about it next week when my mom isn't here, but I'm good with it. I think."

She laughed. "I thought maybe when you felt really good would be a good time to discuss it with you."

"And you did pick that time perfectly." He kissed her nose, and she giggled. "Call them and ask them to come. I think having them here for the holidays would be very nice. Just don't invite my mother. You'll end up with a Christmas bush instead of a Christmas tree, and nothing will ever be the same."

She shook her head. "She can't be that bad."

"I'm just not doing it," he said. "Your family is fine."

"And you're okay with your mother spending Christmas alone?"

He groaned. "I don't want to think about that. Don't play the guilt card on me."

"I'm sure my mom, my sister, and I can keep her from changing things we don't want changed. I just hate the idea of anyone being alone on Christmas."

He sighed. "I guess I do too. I'll invite her, but I don't have to like it."

"No, you don't have to like it. But you have to like my family, okay?"

He grunted, obviously annoyed that she'd talked him into inviting his mother for Christmas. She kissed him and ran the tip of one finger down his chest. "I think we should stop thinking about Christmas and think about the here and now," she said softly.

"Already forgotten."

Chapter Nine

By the end of November, Alexis realized she was pregnant, which was both good and bad in her mind. She wanted children with everything inside her, but she wasn't quite certain that she and Kyle were ready for them. They'd only been married for a few months, and she hadn't even told him she loved him yet.

As she was driving home from the doctor who had confirmed her pregnancy, she called her mother. "Mom, you can't tell anyone until I tell you that it's okay. Promise?"

Her mother squealed. "You're pregnant!"

"You were supposed to let me tell you!" Alexis said, shaking her head. "I'm so excited, and I just had to tell someone. I'm trying to think of the right way to tell Kyle."

Her mother laughed. "Just tell him! He's going to be thrilled."

"I don't know that we've known one another long enough to have a baby, but we are having a baby...I may keep this to myself for a bit."

"I think you should tell him now."

"He's at work. I'll see if telling him this evening feels right."

As she drove, she thought about how well things were going financially. They'd sold off the steers the prior month, and the amount of money received was staggering. She'd never dreamed of that much money, let alone seen in go into her bank account. Of course, what went in wasn't even a fraction of what was already there. Her father must have lived very frugally over the years to have accumulated so much wealth.

She missed him. Though she had no idea how she could possibly miss a man she'd never even met. Everything was so strange, and she wanted it to all feel normal. Maybe it would eventually.

Rebekah was still in the process of slowly decluttering the house, though Alexis was quite happy there were no longer photos of herself smiling down at her from each wall. That had been stranger than she could even express.

When she got home that afternoon, she went straight to her office to work, and was surprised to hear a knock on her office door just moments later. Rebekah usually respected her work time.

Alexis called, "Come in!"

"I found something that I think you'll want," Rebekah said. In her hand was a VHS tape.

"Oh, that thing is ancient!" Alexis said, looking at the tape. "Do they even sell VCRs anymore?"

"There's one in the TV room upstairs," Rebekah said. "This wasn't labeled, so I popped it in, and as soon as I realized what it was, I took it out. It's a message from your father to you."

Alexis accepted the tape and went upstairs to the TV room. She'd really only been upstairs a couple of times, so she had to find the room Rebekah was talking about. She put the tape into the VCR and made sure it was at the beginning.

It took a moment after pushing play for her father to show up on the television screen. "Alexis, I know you don't know me, but my name is Alexander Tobias, and I'm your birth father. Brad has adopted you, and he is treating you as if you are his own child, and I appreciate that. But I don't want you to go your whole life without knowing who I am. Forgive me for using this ancient tape to talk to you, but I never got around to finding a way to record a message on a phone or using a CD."

He ran his fingers through his thick, dark hair in a way she did often. Hearing his voice made her feel so much more for him than mere pictures had.

"You graduated from college yesterday, so I thought it would be a good time to record a message for you. I'm in good health, but you never know when an accident may take you away from this life. I need you to know what having you for a daughter has meant to me all these years."

He cleared his throat, tears shining in his blue eyes, which she then understood. The blue eyes came from him. "I was there for your graduation yesterday, just as I have been for many moments in your life. I'd fly down to Texas for a day and fly back that night, just so I could feel close to you. I attended your high school play. I was there when you gave your valedictory speech in high school. I've been part of your life but you never knew it was me. I was your great aunt Alice, whom you've never met. I did all this because I have a love for you that knows no bounds."

He closed his eyes for a moment before continuing. "I allowed Brad to adopt you and agreed to stay out of your life because of my love for you. I almost hosted you for a summer three years straight, but your mother got scared and backed out every time. As much as I loved your mother, Sara, I love you a thousand times more. I have books filled with pictures of you. I've never held you in my arms, but that doesn't make me any less your father. I hope you understand that I have a love for you that will never stop."

Alexis felt the tears pouring down her face and she brushed them away. Oh, how she wished she'd seen this for the first time before she was pregnant. Now her emotions were like a wound that would never heal, and she wasn't sure she could even watch the whole tape.

"When I die, and I'm hoping that won't be for many years, I will leave my ranch to you with the caveat that you run it yourself and live here. I plan to send you this tape on your twenty-fifth birthday, and invite you to come here and learn the ropes. Maybe you'll even find a man to stand beside you through all of the things you'll need to do as the owner of one of the largest and most successful ranches in this great country of ours."

He took a deep breath. "I hope that you'll agree to come here and spend a few years with me. I would like nothing more. I'll include a letter with my phone number in it along with this tape when I mail it. Please realize that all the decisions I made were to help you not hurt you. I know it's been a different life than you should have lived, and I pray you'll be here with me soon."

The screen went black, and Alexis shook her head as the tears continued to fall. He had died less than a year before her twenty-fifth birthday. "I'm sorry, Dad. You died and my birthday isn't until January. But I'm here, living in this beautiful house of yours and running your ranch. I married a cowboy from Montana, and he's doing a great job with the day-to-day operations. I'm handling the books and the business stuff behind the scenes. I've kept on all of your men except for Joe who decided to retire.

"I'm pregnant. I know you would be thrilled to have another child in place to inherit. I wish I could hug you just once. I feel like I did something wrong for not realizing I wasn't one of Brad's kids." She sighed. "Oh, how I wish you were here!"

She popped the tape out of the VCR and went down to her office, not sure she'd get any work done, but she had to try. She had to keep the ranch going for many years into the future so her father could continue to be proud.

After supper that night, Alexis showed Kyle the tape. "Is this why your eyes are so red?" he asked.

She nodded emphatically. "I watched it and just couldn't stop," she told him. "I want to hug my father just once in my life. Is that too much to ask?"

He took her hand and pulled her down into his lap, wrapping his arms tightly around her. "He loved you."

Alexis smiled, even though the tears were streaming again. "He did. And I would have loved him. I love him now, and he's gone."

Kyle sighed, just holding her close. "I wish I knew what to say, but I have no words."

She nodded, her face against his shoulder. "There really aren't."

When Alexis got up the following morning, she realized she hadn't told Kyle about the baby yet. Her night had been full with the video and with Kyle, but she did need to tell him.

At breakfast, he kept watching her, as if to see if she was going to explode into tears. Finally, he asked, "Do you want me to stay home today? I can have one of the guys do my part."

She shook her head. "No, I'll be fine. I have work I need to get done today as well." Part of her work for the day would be to finish wrapping the gifts she'd gotten for him for Christmas. She'd finally finished her Christmas shopping a few days before, and she was happy to say she wouldn't have to go to any stores during the busy shopping season. Thank God for Amazon.

Rebekah had decided to go to Cambridge, Massachusetts, to be with her son for the holidays, which would leave Alexis with a full house. With her mother and sister there, they could easily manage the meals and cleaning.

All of her spare time would now be focused on getting ready for the invasion of her family and Kyle's mother. Though their first visit with Joyce hadn't been a particularly good one, she expected much better this time with her family there.

She and Rebekah made sure that everything they needed for meals was purchased the week before the holiday, with only a few things that would be coming later.

Growing up, they'd only had artificial Christmas trees, but she decided that she wanted a real one that year, which came with some research not ever having had a real tree in her house before.

They put up the tree the week before Christmas, and she decorated it with ornaments she found among her father's Christmas decorations in the attic. She also had her own special ornaments that she'd collected over the years, and she added those.

Kyle was at work while they put up the tree, but Alexis had already talked to him about it, and he was happy to just let her do it on her own. When they were finished with the tree, Alexis and Rebekah did the outside of the house, adding window clings and huge blow-up Santas and snowmen.

She could see the little hooks all along the front porch where the Christmas lights were supposed to go. Her father even had diagrams along with his decorations, showing exactly where things should go.

By the time they were finished, the house looked like it had come straight from the North Pole to settle in Colorado. It was her first white Christmas, though her mother had told her there'd been one many years ago, this was the first she would remember.

As she tucked all the presents she'd wrapped under the tree, she realized what a beautiful holiday her first Christmas as a married woman would be.

Her family was due to fly in the Thursday before Christmas, which was on a Monday. Kyle's mother would fly in on the Saturday before, giving her time to prepare her mother for what to expect and to have her ready to calm things should something come up.

She planned to make a huge Christmas dinner with turkey, dressing, and all the fixings. It would be a beautiful meal, and she knew her mother and sister would help her get it ready, even if her mother-in-law was not so inclined.

Her family was there on Thursday evening, and she was so happy to see them she couldn't express it. Upon seeing her mother, she started sobbing, scaring Kyle more than a little. "I missed you guys so much!"

Her mom smiled and held her close. "We've missed you too. But you're doing well here. I can see it on your face. By the time I'd been here this long, I was begging Alex to let me stay with my parents for a while."

Wiping away her tears, Alexis smiled. "I wouldn't leave Colorado for anything, but I sure would like to move the family next door so I could see you as often as possible."

They all went into the living room. "Rebekah has one of the rooms upstairs. Don't sleep there, but you guys can choose other rooms."

Her brother grinned. "I want to sleep in the TV room upstairs. That couch is amazing for sleep."

Brittany rolled her eyes. "Only Brent would choose a couch when he could sleep in a nice, cozy bed."

Rebekah had fixed supper, and they all gathered at the table. "If you need anything from me, now's the time to say something," she said. "I leave in the morning."

"Sit with us for supper," Alexis said. "I talk about you to my family all the time, and I'm sure they'd like to get to know you."

Rebekah nodded, moving a plate onto the table for herself.

"Do you need a ride to the airport in the morning?" Alexis asked. "I forgot to ask."

"Your family is here. Stay with them."

"We're all getting our nails done in the morning," Alexis said. "We can drop you off."

"All of you?" Rebekah asked.

"Well, Mom and Brit and me. Kyle will be working, and Dad and Brent will be here at the house." From her seat at the table, Alexis could see the wall where they'd hung various shelves for the kittens, and the two of them were climbing all over them. It was a gift to herself because she loved to just watch them do whatever they wanted.

"If you're going to be in town, that would be great," Rebekah said. "I can bring an Uber home though."

"Call me when you get in, and I'll come if it's convenient."

Rebekah smiled. "Thank you."

Throughout the rest of the meal, they laughed and joked. "Get a cannoli for me while you're in Massachusetts," Brittany told her. "I was there to visit a friend once, and we got the most amazing cannoli."

"I'll try," Rebekah said. "When do you all leave?"

"Wednesday morning," Mom said. "We're staying as long as possible."

"I'll be back Tuesday, so I will bring cannoli if it's at all possible."

"Thank you!" Brittany said. "I haven't been able to stop thinking about the one I got there since I left Massachusetts."

Chapter Ten

When Joyce arrived on Saturday afternoon, she started talking about which decorations needed to come down and which she wanted to hang. As Alexis suspected, her mother put an end to that. "No, this is my daughter's home, and she's happy with the decorations as they are. You can hang what you like in your home."

Joyce glared at Mom while Mom just stared back at her. Finally, Mom said, "My daughter has worked very hard to make everything into what she considered perfect. Why would you insult her by trying to change things?"

Joyce had stomped off and chosen a room upstairs, leaving Alexis and Kyle downstairs with Brittany.

Brent had really been happy with the TV room, and he simply closed the door, letting everyone know that it was his space for the week.

Alexis was in the kitchen making supper for the crowd there. The next night, they'd just have munchies for their meals, but for that night, Alexis was making a huge pot of chicken and dumplings, something her family had always chosen to have around the holidays.

Kyle had been out giving out paychecks and Christmas bonuses. When he arrived home, he looked around for his mother. "Where's Mom?"

"She's mad at my mom and hiding in one of the upstairs rooms."

Kyle's lips quirked with amusement. "Why is she mad?"

"Mom told her she couldn't take down any decorations or put more up."

Kyle closed his eyes and shook his head. "I don't understand why she'd want to do that anyway."

Alexis shrugged. "She wanted things to be perfect for you."

"But you've already made things perfect."

"That's what Mom told her, and she did not like it. Oh, well. We're having chicken and dumplings for supper."

"Oh, that's one of my favorites," he said, leaning down to kiss her quickly. "Are you working alone?"

She nodded. "Mom and Brit went into town to pick up a few last stocking stuffers. They wanted to meet your mom before they got her stocking put together."

"Stockings for adults?" he asked.

She shrugged. "My family has always done that. It's fun."

"Was I supposed to buy things for your stocking?" He felt a moment of absolute panic flood his body.

"Mom's doing that this year as you get to know what we put in the stockings, so you don't have to worry this year. Next year, you probably want to call her for ideas."

"She won't mind?"

"Not at all." She dropped the dumplings she'd been cutting with a pizza cutter into the pot of boiling chicken. "It won't be much longer before supper is ready, but I'll probably let it cook on low for a couple of hours. Everyone can just serve themselves when they're ready."

Joyce came down the stairs and walked straight into the kitchen. "Don't worry, Kyle. I'll make our grilled cheese for our Christmas traditions tonight."

Kyle shook his head. "No thanks, Mom. I'm excited to have chicken and dumplings. You know they've always been a favorite meal of mine."

"But we eat grilled cheese at Christmas time."

"It's okay for me to have something else. You can't force our traditions on a family that has their own."

Joyce stomped out of the room, clearly angry. Again. "Maybe you were right and we shouldn't have invited her," Alexis said softly.

"Don't worry about it. She'll like your traditions."

"I'll make a French toast casserole for breakfast tomorrow. It's too rich for every day, though we all love it, so Mom began making it only on the morning of Christmas Eve. Will your mom get mad at that as well?"

"We have no traditions for breakfast on Christmas Eve, so hopefully, she'll just accept and not throw a fit."

Mom and Brit walked back into the house then. "Chicken and dumplings are on the stove!" Alexis called.

Her mom walked into the kitchen and sniffed deeply. "That's not my recipe," she said. "Good for you for finding one you like better."

"I hope we all like it better," Alexis said. "Joyce is upset that I'm making this and not grilled cheese."

"Grilled cheese? For Christmas?"

"I don't know where she got in her head, we should have that, but I certainly do not think grilled cheese should be on a Christmas weekend menu," Kyle said. "I'll go talk to her."

"I'm sorry," Alexis said softly. He nodded and headed up to his mother.

"Why is she being so difficult?" Brittany asked.

"I think she's afraid she's losing her only child to our family," Alexis said honestly. "Kyle didn't want her to come for Christmas, but I insisted. I didn't think she should have to be alone. No one should be alone on Christmas."

"I'll do what I can to be friends with her," Mom said. "Surely she'll want an ally in the house."

"I hope that works," Alexis said.

They all enjoyed the new chicken and dumplings, and Kyle begged Alexis to make them every day.

"There's no time to make them every day," she said. "These took hours."

"But they're so good."

Joyce sat with her bowl at the end of the table. "They are good," she said, and Alexis smiled at her mother-in-law. "Thank you! This is a new recipe that I found, and I think I love it! Mom's recipe was good, but not as good as this!"

Mom nodded. "Alexis is right. These are the best chicken and dumplings I've ever had."

After supper, Alexis and Brittany did the dishes together, laughing the whole while. "I have our Christmas Eve Eve presents waiting under the tree."

Brittany laughed. "Matching jammies?"

"What else?" Alexis asked. They'd gotten matching pajamas to wear all day Christmas Eve and Christmas Day for as long as Alexis could remember.

So once the dishes were done, they all gathered in the living room, and Brent climbed under the tree, looking for the packages wrapped with snowflake paper. It had been a tradition that all presents which should be opened before Christmas Eve were wrapped in the same paper, so they could easily be sorted from the others.

When Joyce was handed a present that looked much like the others, she frowned. "I didn't get anyone anything for tonight."

Alexis smiled. "Only I did as the hostess this year. It's our family tradition, and I do hope you'll join with us for it."

Joyce smiled, nodding slightly, but Alexis saw a tear in her eye. "New traditions are always good," she said softly.

Kyle who was sitting beside her, put his arm around her. "Merry Christmas, Mom."

Joyce leaned her head against Kyle's shoulder, seeming to have given up on complaining about how things were done. She obviously realized she wouldn't win.

Once all the gifts were passed around, they all opened their presents at the same time. Each pair of pajamas was the same, yet different. All four women got different things. Brittany got shorts and a t-shirt with an elf hat. Joyce got a long nightgown with an elf hat. Mom got a mid-calf nightgown with an elf hat. Alexis got a pair of pajama pants, and a nightshirt that went to her hips....and an elf hat.

Soon, they all had pajamas, and Mom announced it was time to go change into their official Christmas wear. When Joyce came back in her Christmas pajamas, matching everyone else, she seemed much happier.

After everyone was settled around the tree, with Christmas music playing in the background, Mom pulled out a small gift and passed it to Alexis. "I know it's early, but I want us to have time to craft with it while I'm here."

Alexis's mom had always been crafty in a way that Alexis was not. Brittany took after their mother, but Alexis didn't derive the same kind of joy from making things that her mother did.

She took the gift and unwrapped it, revealing four onesies in newborn size, as well as some fabric markers. Alexis stared down at the gift for a moment, feeling heat filling her face. She hadn't found the perfect time to tell Kyle yet, but he'd know for sure now.

"Are you trying to tell me something?" Kyle asked.

Mom's eyes widened, and she whispered, "Sorry, Lexi."

Alexis did her best to make the most out of the moment by taking Kyle's hand and dragging him off to their bedroom. "I was going to tell you Christmas morning, but I guess Mom just blew my surprise."

"How long have you known?" he asked.

She took a deep breath. "About a month."

He looked shocked, and more than a little hurt. "So you've known you were pregnant for a month, and you told your mother, but you didn't bother to tell me?" he asked. "I'm the father!"

She sat down on the bed and looked down at her hands. "I...I just wasn't sure we were ready for a baby yet. Neither of us have even said, 'I love you,' and I thought that should happen first."

"I can't believe you didn't tell me," he said once again.

"I'm so sorry. I know I should have said something sooner, and this isn't the way I wanted you to find out." She looked straight at him. "I love you, and I wanted to tell you on Christmas morning with a gift."

Kyle couldn't believe how badly it hurt that she hadn't told him. "I love you back, but you should have told me. You can't think that all arguments will be solved with you telling me you love me. It's not going to work like that."

She nodded. "I'm aware. I...I messed up, but I thought telling you in a special way was more important than telling you immediately."

He sat down beside her on the side of the bed, taking her hand in his. "We'll settle all this later. For now, we need to go be with family."

Alexis worried she'd ruined their marriage, but he was right. There were guests in the living room, and they needed to pay attention to them.

She plastered a smile on her face, and walked out to her family and his mother, all of them dressed with the same motif, even though their styles of clothing were different.

She sat on the couch beside Kyle, and he kept an arm around her shoulders. She was certain he only did it for appearances, but at least he wasn't shying away from touching her.

They listened to Christmas songs and talked as they did. "What time do we start Monopoly in the morning?" her mother asked.

"I thought we'd play something different," Alexis said. "I found this game called Encore, and you divide into teams. Each team gets a word, and you have to sing a song with that word in it. Then the other team has to do the same. You get to roll if you win with the most songs with the word."

Brittany smiled. "I'm on Lexi's team!"

Alexis grinned at her sister, nodding. "Good."

Brent frowned. "If those two are on the same team, and we're dividing into two teams, I say the other team has five people, and they only have four."

Alexis shook her head at her brother. "You could join us on the winning team. You don't have to try to put together a team that will beat us."

"More fun my way," Brent said.

As they went to bed that night, Alexis waited to hear Kyle say something, anything, about the bombshell. He didn't. Instead, he turned away from her and went to sleep. It was the first time he hadn't at least kissed her goodnight since their wedding, and she turned away from him, feeling the silent tears that slipped down her cheeks.

She was up before anyone else the following day to make the French toast casserole and get the game from the game closet. She only wished she knew where she stood with Kyle. Was he going to hate her forever?

That evening, they opened gifts, and Alexis watched instead of opening any of her own. It was just so much more fun to give gifts than to receive them. Their family had always opened gifts on Christmas Eve, but the stockings were left for Christmas morning.

She'd gotten Kyle new jeans and flannel shirts, knowing that's all he'd wear for work. She'd also gotten him new gloves because his hands had looked like they had been rubbed raw for a while.

From her family, she received maternity clothes from her parents and a necklace from Brittany. From her brother, she'd gotten a Chia Pet. When she opened it, he raised his arms in celebration. "I win!"

This same Chia Pet had been gifted and regifted throughout their family for over five years. If someone realized they were getting the Chia Pet, it would revert to the person who had given it. Alexis sighed. "You win."

When they went to bed that night, Alexis felt content. Maybe Kyle was still angry with her, but the ring he'd given her, with their names and their wedding date inscribed had convinced her things would work out.

Early Christmas morning, she could hear movement in the living room, so she tiptoed out to see what was happening. She needed to start the turkey anyway. It would be a big day of cooking, and she just hoped there would be no complaints about the meal.

She found her brother and sister sitting on the couch. "Finally!" Brit had called when she saw her sister. "Mom said we couldn't wake anyone until you were up."

Alexis laughed. "I'll start the turkey, while you two wake the house," she said.

Their stockings were typically their best gifts. It was impressive the sheer amount of thought their mother had put into the stockings year after year.

The turkey was in the oven when Kyle joined the rest of them in the living room. "Sorry. Extra sleepy."

Alexis smiled. "Me too! But the turkey is in the oven, and I'm hoping I'll have help with the rest of the fixings."

"I've got mashed potatoes," Brittany offered.

"I'm doing the dressing," Mom said.

"I can make green bean casserole," Joyce said.

"Perfect. And I'm making Butterfinger pie, which I know isn't traditional, but it sure sounds good."

"Already getting cravings?" Brittany asked.

Alexis didn't respond, not wanting to upset Kyle more than he already was. Brent stood and started to grab stockings. Joyce looked surprised when she received one, but she smiled. "I've forgotten what being part of a big family is like for Christmas," she said softly. "It's been just Kyle and me for so long."

"All right," Brent said as he took the last stocking for himself. "When I yell go, we all dig in."

The next few minutes were chaos as they each opened the small wrapped gifts inside their stockings. Alexis half-watched Kyle waiting until he found the special gift she'd found for him. It was a picture frame, with her sonogram picture inside it. And on the frame, it said,

"To the best daddy a child could ask for." There were ponies and horseshoes decorating the frame.

Kyle looked at it for a moment, and he turned to Alexis, pulling her into his arms and kissing her. "This would have had a lot more impact if I hadn't already known."

She nodded. "I'm sorry you found out how you did, but I'm so glad you know now."

He nodded, tears filling his eyes. She smiled, putting his hand over her belly, which wasn't showing yet at all.

When all the stockings had been opened, Joyce shook her head. "Thank you all for letting me be part of Christmas with you. I hope we'll do this again, and I'll still be invited."

Alexis smiled at Joyce. "Of course, you will. You're family."

That night, after the onesies had been decorated, and the family had enjoyed themselves and eaten the meal they'd cooked together, he'd pulled her into his arms. "Today was perfect. I'm sorry I reacted so badly to the news of the baby."

Alexis smiled. "As long as you're happy that he or she is coming, then I'm fine with how you reacted."

He leaned down and kissed her. "How could I not be happy when I love you more than I ever dreamed I could?"

Epilogue

Six months later, Alexis sat up in her hospital bed, holding their tiny son. "He looks like you," she said.

"I think he looks like your father," Kyle replied.

"Maybe."

"When does your mom get here to help?"

"She wants to be in town when I'm released from the hospital. Then she can help me through the first couple of weeks of motherhood."

"My mom wants to come when she leaves."

"And she should," Alexis said. "It's her grandson."

"You sure?" he asked.

She nodded. "I'm positive. I'm just glad Rebekah is doing all she does. I don't have to worry about not having supper ready on time or about dirty diapers. The house will still run smoothly."

"Other than our midnight wake-up calls," he said, grinning.

"And that's what the moms are for."

"Thanks for giving me a son," he said softly. "Are we still going with Alexander Kyle?"

She nodded. "Alex deserves credit for bringing us together."

"I agree. He really does."